WITH EVERY

HE TOOK MY SOUL

By Niecie Hammond

Disclaimer
This book contains adult language, it is intended for mature audiences ages 18 years and older. This is a fictional book where I have changed some names to protect individual's privacy.

All rights reserved. No part of this book may be reproduced or used in any manner without the prior written permission of the copyright owner, except for the use of brief quotations in a book review.

To request permissions, contact the publisher at: nelsonniecie@gmail.com

Edited by: Amy VWrite

Cover art by: Amyra Washington

WITH EVERY BREATH HE TOOK MY SOUL,

Copyright ©2021 by Niecie Hammond

All Rights Reserved

I dedicate this book to my brother Paul.

A Brother's Love, a Mother's Son (Paul)

You had us racing, doing your dishes. Man, we didn't care because we wanted those cookies. You would say, "First one finished would win." We all jump in on the count of 3. You always had a grin. With a smile, you laughed because inside, you knew we all would win a prize. A brother's love is truly amazing. You came up with nicknames that made us laugh. We joked. We cried as we all lined up to feel the raft. A mother's son, you will always be a brother that kept us together. Man, that was neat. As we look back on all that we shared, through it all, your love was always there. I can hear you say don't cry for me. I'm okay... Tell Mommy I love her, and don't forget to play your numbers. You will win. You'll see. Tell my brother, Man, check out my wings. It's real gold. I'm flying now. Tell my sisters I love them. Don't worry... You ready? On the count of 3, I'm finally free.

We love you Paul. Yes, you win the prize this time. You fly, brother, fly high...

CONTENTS

INTRODUCTION 1

CHAPTER 1: THE WAIT 3

CHAPTER 2: TRUSTING WHAT WASN'T THERE 22

CHAPTER 3: LOSING YOURSELF 39

CHAPTER 4: Loving in the Midst of the Storm 63

CHAPTER 5: ALONG CAME THE SUN WITH THE RAIN 80

CHAPTER 6 GOODBYE 94

CHAPTER 7: I AM ENOUGH 115

CHAPTER 8: ONLY GOD 140

CHAPTER 9: THE RELEASE 170

CHAPTER 10: SURRENDERING TO FORGIVENESS 190

ACKNOWLEDGEMENTS 216

BIOGRAPHY 219

INTRODUCTION

Angel is at home waiting on Brian to return from his business trip. Angel has her condo where she stays when she has to work because Brian's house is further away from, her job. Angel moved in with Brian a couple of months ago, it wasn't easy for Angel to make that decision because of Brian's pass. Angel is a doctor working on her master's degree in Psychology. She works long hours but still finds time to spend with the love of her life. Brian is an owner of 3 major sports gym where he is trying to have his own youth sports camp. Brian and Angel live in ATL, Angel is thinking back when she would always be waiting on Brian back in the pass. Angel and Brian have gone through a lot of trials in the pass, Angel is trying to put the pass behind her and focus on the future. Angel suffered a lot with Brian but yet her faith remain strong, she endured a lot of pain with dating Brian. Both Brian and Angel have their own demons that they try to put to rest. With everything that they have been through both of them struggle with the pass, the present but with God they manage to keep strong and love each other even when they find it hard to love their selves. Angel is remembering the pass that causes her to be afraid of the present she goes by what Brian is showing her now. Angel awaits patiently as she thinks back to the pass that lead Brian and her to their future.

CHAPTER 1:

THE WAIT

It has been a long day for Angel. The time has come and gone. She is anxious to finally be able to spend time with Brian, but she waits patiently for him to arrive. It has truly been a very trying time for Brian and Angel. She never thought they would have made it this far with all that they have gone through.

She remembers it all—some she wishes she could forget because of all the pain it involved, but with pain came growth, and those two made it through the storms. Angel sits as she thinks back to their first encounter.

Her daughter, Mary, thought it would be a good ideal to help her mom out with finding a man. Mary thought it was time since her and her brothers Timothy, Matthew, and Johnathan were all grown now. Mary tells Angel, "I am going to put you on a dating site to find a man." Now, Angel did not know much about these dating sites. Because of her job, she really didn't get out much or entertain certain people. Being a doctor made it very hard for Angel to find a good man. So, Angel went along with the ideal of her daughter. She added pictures of herself, and it took off from there. She was hooked. Angel was getting likes, she was swiping right, but there was more swiping left then right. Out of all the men, she found 5 promising candidates. She first started talking to Ben, who OMG just was very handsome, but when he started talking, he was a pervert. He asked her how big her nipples were, and Angel could not believe this. She was like what the hell did her daughter sign her up on. Angel quickly dismissed Ben.

Then there was Tony, who was nice looking, but the conversation was not really there. Angel loved to have a good conversation. She just went on down the line till she came across Brian. His profile was pretty interesting. He had photos up of himself in a suit. He had shown where he wrote a book and had these famous people in the background. But what got her attention was what Brian had written on his profile. Angel still remembers it by heart. He wanted a woman who was very, very attractive, classy but a little sassy. Family oriented and had time. She was like, wow, that is her. She was like, okay God, this must be the one. Angel was also drawn to the emptiness he had in his eyes. She wanted to know what his story was. Brian reached out to her immediately, he told her she was very attractive. She giggled and said, "Thank you, sir." She always referred to every male as sir out of respect.

Brian told her he was not going to be on this site for long, so he wondered if he could get her phone number. Angel knew that had to be a lie because all the guys said that, so she was like, yeah, right, but she gave him her number because she was very curious who this Brian was; she just felt something inside. He called her immediately, he told her that texting was so interpersonal that he wanted to call her and talk to her. But instead, Brian video messaged her. She was just about to get in the shower. She knew he would do that. Brian wanted to make sure he was not getting catfished. Brian and Angel talked and talked. It was so nice. Angel thought it was so good to finally have a man to talk to. Angel had her secrets that scared her, she thought about pushing Brian away. Brian was not going to let Angel go anywhere. He would call her late at night just to hear her voice. Angel loved that about him, it made her want to know more and more about him. Angel was kind of sad because this was the month when she had lost her oldest brother.

Angel had two brothers; her oldest brother died. Peter Jr. had died at age 53, 2 years ago of a massive heart attack. It still hurts Angel from this day. Peter protected Angel. She remembers being about 16 years of age when her mother had gotten mad at her and her younger brother Ralph. Angel and Ralph had found their mother's gun, and they pretended to rob their older sister Roxanne. Roxanne was the oldest sister. Leslie was the younger sister. Angel was a true middle child; they were not lying when they say the middle child catches hell. Well Angel saw her share of hell. Roxanne had told on Angel and Ralph to their mother about them playing with her gun. Her mother Gladys. Gladys worked on the military base as a cook. Angel's parents had divorced when she was about 6. She remembers her dad and mom fighting like crazy. Her dad was Peter Sr. He was in the military, so he was gone a lot but came back with a bad drinking problem, he would be very angry. Angel was too young to really understand what was going on or who was really the bad parent. There was the one time she remembers her dad throwing her mom out the glass door where she fell through then she ran away. Angel did not see her again for a while. They always made jokes as a kid. They never took things seriously. Angel thought they just made everything out to be a game. Angel thinks that is why when she was being abused by her mother, no one took it seriously because they grew up seeing it all the time. Gladys came home.

Roxanne said, "Mommy, Ralph and Angel had your gun and were playing with it. They pointed it at me."

Gladys was pissed off, so she got the belt. She took Ralph into the other room. She started whipping him, she hit Ralph 5 times, and then it was Angel's turn. Angel believed she deserved the whipping, so she took her turn. Gladys started whipping and whipping. Before you knew it, Angel was bleeding. There were no more tears she could cry. What was supposed to be a whipping became a beating of hate. It was like Gladys was taking all her hate for Angel out on her; she did not know why her mother hated her so much as she continued to beat her. Peter was so enraged that he ran in the room and told Gladys she was killing her and to stop, but Gladys would not. She was mad that Peter even came into the room that she began to run for him. Peter called her a bitch and ran out the house. He saved Angel even though he sacrificed himself. Angel never forgot that day. Peter was a little slow because Gladys had him when she was 16, she was drinking a lot. Gladys was a wild child back in her days. Night came and no Peter. Angel was so scared she blamed herself for Peter leaving. Peter finally came home. No one knew where he went. We were just happy he was home. Roxanne blamed herself; she said she should have never told mommy on Angel and Ralph.

Brian finally returns home; Angel is overjoyed because he has been away for a week on a business conference. Brian owns his own fitness center where he specializes in explosive high-tech training for successful athletes and children of the future who are looking to become the best or the next best thing. Angel admires Brian. He is good at what he does. Angel remembers the first time coming to his gym to visit him. She was so nervous but excited to see what he did to just see him work with the men, women, and children. Brian is very passionate about what he does. Angel had no idea what all went into Brian's training sessions.

He was sitting in the chair outside the lobby area waiting on her. He showed her around the place. Of course, he could not keep his hands off her. His first client came in. Angel sat out in the lobby Brian texted her. He asked her if she wanted to come in and watch him. She was very happy that he asked. Angel watched as he trained the little boy. She was just blown away. He was really good at what he did. She really loved this man. He was into making sure the young boy got everything he could teach him. It was like he was that little boy; he was teaching him what he wanted his dad to teach him. He pushed him very hard, but the boy did not mind; he just did whatever Coach B told him. Angel did not stay long. It was Brian's last client, so he was getting ready to leave too. Brian kissed Angel bye. Angel went home, she was all smiles; she still could feel Brian's touch. She thought back to the first time Brian came over, how the conversation on the phone went. Angel remembered him texting, calling her all the time. He was working two jobs when she first met him. Brian was driving for a trucking company that delivered liquor to different companies. He really did not like it, but he did not have that many client's business was slow. He needed extra money, so he was busting his butt doing both. Brian always found time to slip in a call or text or two to Angel to let her know she was on his mind. She loved hearing from Brian. He made her smile on the inside. They had been on the phone talking for about a month before they finally met up on a date. Angel was really scared to open herself up to Brian. She was trying to keep her past from him, that hurt little girl. They would talk late nights, Angel loved hearing Brian's voice on the phone. He made her feel so warm inside she was able to sleep through the night. The night brought back painful memories for Angel, that little girl would run wild in her dreams.

There is this little girl that was lost. She was searching for love because with the word love came rejection, pain, and confusion. All her life growing up, she had to be strong. She had to endure so much pain that it nearly took her life; she wanted to die. The word love was so horrible to her that when she would hear it, it would make her sick to her stomach. She would vow to never ever feel love or speak love. The struggles she faced with her mother physically and mentally abusing her, she could not understand why her, when there were other siblings. She wanted her mother's love, she wanted to feel what people say love is supposed to feel like. She kept trying to please everyone including her mother. Beating after beating, nights of being awakened to perform for her mother's male friends, she grew up hating what she saw in the mirror. Even now that little girl finds at times when she looks in the mirror imperfection. She thought if she were perfect, that her mother would love her and everyone else would too! Each day became a challenge for this little girl at age 8. She was made to walk to school because she missed her bus. It truly was not a walk an eight-year-old was to take. The highways and across busy streets, it was a five mile walk if she was able to walk it alone. But God or the devil saw that it was truly not a walk for her to take alone. She was picked up by a white man in a red car. He had beer cans and bottles everywhere. He had a brown beard with medium brown hair. He looked kind of dirty. The little girl was scared. The little girl had on her favorite dress; it was white with green leaves on it, it was her favorite because her grandmother who she knew loved her got it for her. She had on white tights with her black Easter shoes. She was so happy even knowing she was being made to walk to school. That happiness soon faded to tears of hurt of fear and wonder of what is going to happen if her mom found out that this man touched her where no man should ever touch. What would her mother do if she finds out that he took her hand and made her feel what was growing in between his legs. She remembers him asking her if she had hair down there. She cried even harder and began to pray to God to please help her. The little girl really did not know God, but she had to believe in something, so someone could help her. He grabbed her hand and pulled out his white, hard penis. He made her grab it. She cried even more. She tried to pull her hand away, but he would not let her. She kept crying, praying and finally he let go of her hand. He told her to hush her mouth! That he would take her to school.

She must promise to never tell a soul. She promised, and she ran out the car as he pulled up to the door. She ran and ran and never looked back. The little girl walked in the school building. She took a deep breath as she greeted everyone with a smile that she learned how to wear all too well. No one saw that hurt little girl or the tears she hid. She always wore a smile on the outside, so no one would know that one day she wanted to die.

Angel jumps in Brian's arms. She wanted to erase that memory of that day the white man came to play. She loved being in his arms; she always felt so safe. Brian just gives her that little smile, he holds her so tight; he always acts like she was too heavy to hold up. Brian was a strong man. He was well in shape; his chest was so broad, his arms were very well formed, and he could fill out an extra-large T-shirt that made Angel's day. Brian had the sexiest butt she had ever seen. His entire body could be on a GQ magazine. He was her King, and she felt so lucky to have him. Angel thinks back to their first date. She was like a little girl, trying to make sure she looked her best. She was so scared she worried he would not like her; she was so much older than him. For now, Angel was just happy he was home. She loved missing him but loved having him

home with her. The past made her very thankful for the time together.

Angel wondered how it was going to be when her and Brian would finally meet face to face, how nervous she was because it has truly been a while since she had a man. That little girl in her was running wild, she did not know if she would even be able to go out. November 16, a Saturday was when they were supposed to go out, but Friday Brian did not call Angel, which made her mad because he always called her. Angel did not really understand at the time what it all involved for Brian to run his own business; she just wanted to hear his voice. So, when Saturday came, she ignored his text and then his call, but later that night, she could not take it, so she texted him a very long text about how she felt, but deep inside that little girl was trying to find a way to protect herself, so she was pushing Brian away. Brian was not having it. He called her Sunday morning and asked if he could call her after church, so he could reread her text to get a better understanding of what she was saying. Angel thought about Brian calling her back. She had it all planned out; she was just going to not even bother with being with him. Angel figured it would be for the best because she was not ready to let anyone into her heart, she was so afraid of the way she was already feeling about

Brian. Church had ended. Angel was driving over to her sister's house to just clear her head and sit with her sister. Brian called her, and they began to talk. Angel said she was not trying to have a disagreement. Brian told her they were not having a disagreement, that they were two people trying to get to know one another, so she might as well take off her running shoes because she wasn't going anywhere. Angel smiled, she was moved by what Brian had said, then he asked her if she was his baby. She replied yes, Angel did not really think about it. She was just going on her emotions; she just felt so good just hearing his voice. December 22 was their first date. Angel was having a hard time because that is the day that Peter had passed. She was trying to find peace with Brian. Angel and Brian were to meet up at the movie theater. Angel arrived there first, not sure what to expect. She was so nervous, wondering if he was going to like her. She could barely control her thoughts, her emotions. The little girl inside her started to get scared, worried about if he touched her what she would feel. Brian was running a little late because he had put the wrong address in his GPS when he was leaving his other job. So, Angel waited patiently but was anxious. Brian finally arrived, he just grabbed her in his arms like he already knew her. Angel was filled with all these emotions; she did not know how she was going to explain to him that she did not know what love was or how it felt. She was lost for words, and her breath was taken away. She wanted to stay in his arms. It felt so safe, she never felt this before. Angel wanted to cry, but she did not. They went into the movie theater where they sat. Brian could not keep his eyes off her as he told her, "I'm going to marry you." Angel thought, yeah, right and laughed, but Brian leaned over and kissed her to assure her he meant what he said. Brian told her that in a year and a half he was going to marry her. Brian asked Angel if she wanted him to propose on Valentine's Day or her birthday. Angel's birthday was February 15, so she picked her birthday. She was very flattered but still did not believe him. Brian did not even watch the movie. He would doze off, only to wake up and begin kissing Angel again and again. Angel was just filled with joy. They left the movie and walked to her truck, where they sat in the back seat as they began to talk. He leaned over so gently and kissed her lips. He made his way down to her neck. Angel was overjoyed with this moistness that was coming from in between her legs that it scared her; she told him to stop but never sharing what had taken place between her legs. Brian kissed her again. She could feel her spirit leave her body as she floated. It felt amazing. Angel had never had that happened. Angel tells Brian, "Okay, I must leave now. We must go." Brian laughed as he looked her in her eyes with those sad, lonely eyes he had. She would wonder what he was thinking, what his story was, what he was hiding? Brian did not want to leave, but he was tired, and he thought Angel would let him come over. Angel was not ready for Brian to come over to her place, but she knew he wanted to. They say goodbye. Angel was just smiling. She thought, Finally, please God let him be the one.

Angel looks at Brian now. She still feels the same feelings she did back then. Brian is tired from all the lectures and training he did while he was away. He went upstairs to take a hot shower; Angel was eager to follow him because she longed for his touch, to feel him inside of her. Angel goes and cooks Brian something to eat, she gets him a nice cold beer, so he could relax. Angel loves waiting on Brian; that is something that was instilled in her, and she did not mind. Brian loved that about her as well as the attention she gave him. She submitted herself to him, and he loved her for that. Brian would spoil her and protect and provide for her. She thought it is the least she could do is make him feel wanted and like a king. Angel thinks back to the first time Brian ever really touched her.

Angel is home now. She cannot stop feeling Brian's presence on her entire body as she remembers what just took place in the back seat of her BMW, how wonderful he made her feel. She loved kissing Brian, having him touch her. He was so gentle. The way her body was responding to his ever so gentle touch, she craved more, but Angel was still afraid of what will come with more. Angel wonders what was coming out of her that made her panties so wet. She could not believe she had never experienced such pleasure before. Angel wondered what Brian thought, what was he feeling. Was he feeling her too, or was she just like everyone else to him? Angel realized she really did not know anything about him. Brian really did not talk that much. Angel knew that Brian loved to touch her and kiss her. That made her feel special. She wonders if she made him feel special too. Angel wanted more than just touching and kissing; she wanted that connection, communication. Angel and Brian would talk on the phone for hours sometimes, and other times Brian would just shoot her a good morning text or sneak in calls in between his breaks. Angel loved that it was nice to be able to communicate and share he made her feel appreciated.

Brian is in the shower. Angel can see his hard, sexy body through the shower glass doors. She watches as the

water drips down from his body. She sees his big dick just hanging there, waiting for her to come in. She gets so excited that she cannot wait. Angel enters the shower. She had forgotten all about the food and beer. She would be his food and relaxation. Angel can tell that Brian was just as honored for her presence; he still looks at Angel in awe. He cannot believe at times that this body of hers belongs to a 50-year-old woman. Angel was very much in shape; she did not really look her age. Brian loved her body; he could never resist it. Brian grabbed her, kissed her so strongly that Angel just melted away like she always does. Brian wanted to make love to her, so he turned off the water, picked her up, and he took her to the bed. Angel loved when Brian would be so anxious it meant he longed for her when he makes love to her it is always magical. Angel still remembers the first time.

Brian would call late at night sometimes. It was like he would wake up and think about Angel. He would just say, "Baby, I miss you." Then he would go back to sleep. Brian would always ask to come over Angel's house. Angel would always say, "One day." Brian laughed, and he just continued to ask to come over, until that one day came. Angel knew she wanted Brian just as much as he wanted her, but that little girl in her was afraid. She remembers that horrible day when her innocence was taken away. *There was blood between her legs as he held her down. He placed a pillow over her face and told her if she screamed, he would cut her throat. The little girl could hear the music playing louder and louder. She got caught up in the melody of the sense of peace. The little girl closed her eyes. She floated away dreaming of heaven. She felt her spirit lift, she felt no more pain; she did not even hear herself scream. The little girl did not remember what had just taken place. He grabbed her by the hand and escorted her to his car. The little girl was home now, sitting in her bed, wondering if this made her a woman now. Was this how love felt? She called her best friend, told her the good news only to hear her friend on the phone crying as she yelled, "You were RAPED!" RAPED rang loudly in her ears as she sat there in tears, yelling once again, "Why, God? Why does the pain continue to grow, and why must I suffer so much? I just want to be loved but now I cannot even feel love." The little girl was eighteen, still a virgin, still innocent. Now she was dirty, but still had no idea what love was or is.*

Brian was at the front door. Angel remembers being so excited but nervous because the little girl was going crazy with fear. She wanted him, but the memories of eighteen rang loud in her ear. Angel knew nothing at that time on how to please or love a man. How was she going to tell him that she is different? She is new. How does she tell him how he is making her body feel, how his voice excites her? Angel opens the door, and Brian is standing there with a little smirk on his face. He grabs her, he hugs her so tight; Angel wants to kiss him so badly, to have his lips on hers. She longs for them like bees to honey. She wanted more and more of him. Angel is shaking but loved what he was doing to her. They only talk for a little bit before he is touching her body. Brian tells her to sit on his lap. She is very eager to do so, she is like a little kid in the candy store, wanting to try everything. Brian is kissing Angel so softly, very passionate. He strokes her between her legs, and she can feel the same stuff coming out like before but more. She tells him to stop because she was not sure if this was pee or what it is, but Angel still wanted Brian to keep going because it was amazing to her. She could feel herself slipping away, she had no control over her body or mind. She was overtaken by this amazing feeling. Brian then told her to open her mouth. He began to breathe into her, and she felt every bad thing leave her body as he sucked out the air in her. It was like he was removing every bad feeling she ever endured. Angel was overwhelmed with excitement that she wanted to cry. As her body started to shake, she felt her legs tingle from what was pouring out in between her legs; it was so magical that Angel wanted more of Brian. She felt her body shaking. She was crying out, but no words left her mouth, but there were tears of joy. Angel could not breathe; she felt herself about to pass out.

Angel lays there thinking about how Brian still makes her feel so amazing, the pleasure he gives.

Brian begins to enter her. Angel is so full of excitement; it does not take long for her to cum. She just pours out. She could feel the wetness run down her legs. Brian always loved that about Angel, and he loved when he made her squirt. Angel did not like it because it was so messy, but she enjoyed the feeling that came with the wetness. Brian has a very nice size dick that Angel at first could barely even take, but he was always gentle and still is as he whispers in her ear, "I love you." They both lay in each other's arms and fall asleep.

CHAPTER 2:
TRUSTING WHAT WASN'T THERE

Brian is heading out to work. He has 3 gyms that he is running, and he has to check all of them to make sure his trainers are getting what they need to make sure business is running smoothly. Angel just admires Brian because he always worked hard. Well, she thought he was back in the day. It was hard for Angel. She remembers Brian and all those times he said he was working, how he did not have time. He always made it like he was so busy. Brian was a very quiet man. Angel remembers back when they started seeing each other Brian would rarely talk; he just loved kissing and touching Angel.

Brian would call or text just about all the time. They would be on the phone for hours before he would come over. Angel always wondered why he would never come over early, but Brian would always say he had to work. Angel would always be waiting on the next time to see Brian because he barely came over. They lived, like, 35 minutes away from each other. Angel would always tell Brian she could come to him. Brian would always say he did not want her out driving so late. Angel thought that was very protective of Brian and caring. Angel also thought maybe he was hiding something from her; she never really stayed focused on the negative because it made her sad. Angel just wanted to believe what Brian said and keep it moving. She knew that time would tell the truth; it always does.

Angel is getting dressed now for work herself. She is an ER Trauma doctor. She is on the night shift. Brian loved that about Angel how caring she was and that she was a doctor he was so proud of her. Brian did not like that hours that Angel had to work, he wanted to somehow be the provider and give Angel everything she desire because he felt she deserved it. Angel was also going to school for her master's in psychology she wanted to retire and work as a sports psychologist. Brian would just give Angel all the support he could because he knew what she does isn't easy for her. Brian has four children and three baby moms. He has a set of twins, a boy James and a girl Janice, both are 3 years of age. Brian had found out that James was autistic, it broke Brian's heart, but he just kept pushing. Brian never shares his true feelings. You must either catch him on one of his weak days, or just make him open up,

but he is doing so much better with sharing now. Back in the past, Angel had to question him to get anything out of him at times. Angel thinks back to the time when she finally met Brian's oldest son and the twins.

Brian's oldest son was named Jeff. He had started college at North Georgia State University. The campus was just 5 miles from Angel's apartment. Brian was bringing Jeff down along with the twins to get Jeff's ID card that he needed when he did his move in, so they agreed to meet up at the Waffle House down from Angel's apartment. Angel was so nervous because she wanted Brian's son to like her. Angel's son Matthew his girlfriend Isabel was over at the house, so she brought her with her. Angel pulls up to the Waffle House, jumps out the truck, and walks in. Brian jumps up, greets her with a hug and a kiss, he introduces her to Jeff. Jeff just looks at Angel and says hello. Angel was like he sure does have his daddy's height and he was very polite. The twins were in the highchairs just looking. The waitress comes over and immediately says you cannot be the grandma; Angel was like how did she know she is a grandma? Angel smiled. Angel sits down right beside Jeff, and Isabel sits across from them. Angel asked Jeff what was the waitress talking about, Jeff said he had no idea. Then Angel just figured it out the waitress must have thought that Brian was the grandpa and Jeff was the father of the twins. Jeff and Angel laughed at the idea of Brian looking old and Angel looking young. Angel was just happy to finally meet at least 3 of his children. His oldest daughter Janea' stayed in Middle Georgia that was a little further away.

Angel walked out the house to go to work. Brian had called her and told her to have a safe night. He would be waiting for her when she got home. Angel's schedule was crazy. She worked from 6:00 p.m. till 6:00 a.m., 12 hours so when she worked, she rarely saw Brian because he was leaving the house at 8:00 a.m. to go to work. But when she had her days off, they would enjoy time out, he would take her out to dinner and maybe a movie or something they would just enjoy whatever. Angel had moved in with Brian because he had asked her to move in. Brian wanted Angel closer to him since he had the twins. Angel didn't mind making that sacrifice. Angel was scared at first because of the past, but she told him she would only move in with him if they bought another house and she was able to meet Elizabeth the twin's mother. Angel felt it was time because she would be picking the twins up at times. Brian had arranged for them to meet. Angel and Elizabeth sat down and talked at a restaurant; the conversation went well. Elizabeth was a very strong women, she just fell in love with the wrong man who she gave birth to 12 children. Angel felt sorry for her because she could only imagine being young and trusting a man who you believed would love you forever only to leave you with a house full of babies. Brian had become her other children stand in dad. Angel loved that about Brian his caring heart, he just didn't care about his two he also helped with the other children Elizabeth had. Angel wanted Elizabeth to know that she was not going to stop Brian from helping her, she hoped she could help her as well. Angel wanted a fresh start, a new beginning with their memories so meeting Elizabeth and moving would be good for them. Brian agreed, so they found a nice house still close to Elizabeth, so they both can still help and pick the twins up. Brian wanted to eventually get the twins, so Angel and he were getting things in order, so they could get the twins' full-time.

It wasn't long before Brian started being distant. Angel and he used to talk almost every day, sometimes twice a day, they would talk late on the phone and just share. Time went on. Brian suddenly became distant, no phone calls, no texts, nothing. Angel got worried. She would call text, even video messaged him, but he was not answering she worried something was wrong. Finally, Brian answered. He said he was fine; he just had a lot going on. Brian never shared much with Angel. He kept a lot to himself, it bother Angel a lot she felt like he left her out. Angel wanted Brian to trust her. Angel knew that he must be having a hard time and didn't want her to know his problems, so he just kept things to himself. Time went on. Brian was acting kind of different. Angel could not make out what was going on. But she continues to embrace what they had shared. Angel just figured it was either something with business or the twin's mom. Angel just tried to push positive energy Brian's way. She would just text him some motivational quotes to uplift his spirits to let him know she was here for him.

Time was always a problem to Angel because Brian seems to start losing time. He hardly wanted to come over. Angel just believed he was busy, she just kept being supportive. She didn't know what else she could do because Brian wasn't talking to her. Angel just went on with her days, and just hoped that whatever Brian was going through it would pass.

Angel would go faithfully every year for her annual physical, making sure she was still healthy and cancer free. Angel was diagnosed with stomach cancer in 2009. It changed her entire life; she was in nursing school at that time. Angel had to work and go to school, so she could give her children a better life. Their dad was not involved in their life, so it was Angel who had to provide for them. By now she and Brian have been dating about 9 months. Everything seems to be okay besides Brian being a little distant. Angel was able to talk with Brian from time to time. He would shoot her a text, saying he loved her and calling her Mrs. Ward. That gave Angel hope. It was around June when Brian had video messaged Angel. He was laid up in his bed, looking very sad. It looked as though he had been crying. Angel asked him what was going on as she had not heard from him in a week. Brian just assured her all was ok. He was dealing with financial stuff and personal stuff. Brian was really trying hard to make it; his house was in foreclosure as he started to open up to Angel more about his personal stuff. He was barely making it, but Angel believed he was hiding more. Angel told Brian, "I feel like you are not telling me something." Brian was like, "What?" Angel did not know, but she just had this bad feeling in her gut.

Angel jumps up and realizes it's getting late, and she had not cooked anything; Brian should be home soon. Brian always loved Angel's cooking. He said she was the best out of all the women he dated, even his ex-wife

cooking. Brian comes home excited with good news. Brian was able to get another pro athlete to join his gym and get sponsored. He is looking to open a camp for the youth to have his own Youth Push and Power Conditioning Camp. It would be awesome for him for us Angel thought.

Angel watches as Brian tells her all the details on how he was able to get the pro athlete to join his gym. Angel enjoys hearing Brian tell his stories. She tries to help out when she is off at some of his locations, with training some of the women's classes. Brian wants her to be more involved with the business. Angel remembers when he barely even shared the business with her. He would never let her help. She offered, but he would say he was good. She now knows why he did not want her there because of the secrets he was hiding. Brian had to make sure he had all his paperwork in order, so Angel was able to help with that stuff because she was a perfectionist, and she loved things to be in order. Angel had to make sure any new person had gotten a physical to make sure they were fit to train, so they would not sue Brian for anything. Angel would also put the finance in a spreadsheet, so Brian could keep track with payments, she also did his payroll at times to be second eyes. Angel enjoyed helping Brian with the business; it made her feel a part of it, and it kept them

connected. Angel was thinking back to the day she went to the doctors for her physical. How Brian was so distant at first and then came around.

Angel remembers being like a little girl sitting in the doctor's office talking to Brian, he had asked her why she was there. Angel told him, "For my annual checkup. I have to get checked regularly to see if my cancer cells have grown back. Brian said, "Okay, I just want to make sure you are ok." Angel was sitting in the doctor's office, taking pictures, sending them to Brian. Angel was so happy just to finally hear his voice again. Dr. Kim asked Angel if she wanted to get blood work and get tested for HIV and STDs. Angel did not think nothing of it; she always gets tested even knowing she did not have nothing. Ever since Angel has been having sex with Brian, she would get these yeast infections all the time. It drove her crazy. She was very in tune with her body, so she figured it was because Brian was very well in size. Dr. Kim told her to make sure Brian washes his hands, and they both laughed. Angel has been seeing Dr. Kim for years, so she was very aware of Angel's body, she gave her some medicine for the yeast infection, she told Angel that, "Yes, the size of Brian is causing you to tear some, that it is making it sensitive, so he needs to be gentle." Angel did not know how much gentler Brian could be because he was already gentle. Angel just figured with time she would get used to it. About two weeks later after Brian was distant, he came over. He surprised Angel and told her to get dressed because he was taking her out. Angel was on cloud 9 because they have not been out for a while. Most of the time Brian would come over late, and they would just lay together. Angel did not really like that, she liked it, but she wanted to go out at times too. She figured because Brian was so busy, she just enjoyed having him there with her. Angel gets dressed; they head out. He does not tell her where they are going; he wanted to surprise her. They end up at Andretti's. Brian walked around with his tight shirt and his nice shorts. Angel thought he looked so handsome even though he did not shave, but he was not in sweatpants, so she was happy about that. Angel just had on shorts and a tank top. They walked around; Brian took her back to an area where he wanted to take pictures. Angel was so surprised about that as most men do not take the pictures. It's always the women, so Angel felt very special. Angel still thinks about those pictures; she smiles every time she looks at them, she remembers how happy she was at that moment and night. Angel did not realize how very protective Brian is over her. They went to go ride the go-carts; Angel had got hit by another driver. Brian was so worried that he stopped his car and got out just to try to check on Angel. Angel thought that was so cute, Angel ended up beating Brian on the race cars. They played the shooting game, and Brian beat Angel by 3 points. Angel was truly enjoying this night. Seeing Brian smile and laugh just made her happy. They go get something to eat afterwards then head home. Angel was so happy, feeling loved. As soon as they get in Angel's apartment, Brian looks at her and kisses her. Angel just melts away. Brian takes her so gently and lays her on the living room floor; Angel had this very soft fluffy carpet. Brian lays her down and begins to remove her clothes. Angel is so excited; she could feel the moistness begin to flow from her legs. It felt like the first time, Angel did not know why she was so nervous, but she was. Brian just looked at her differently. He was so passionate and very loving. He kissed her everywhere, Angel just spilled out all of her juices her pussy was so wet and tingling. Brian licked her wet pussy, and Angel cried out, "Oh my God, Brian, I love you so much!" she felt the tears begin to fall. He held her tighter and began licking even more. She was so wet the carpet was soaked, but she did not care because what she was feeling was truly amazing. Brian gently lays on Angel and looks at her in her eyes. Angel looks back; she could see those sad, lonely eyes of Brian. She could feel his love for the first time. As Brian places his big hard dick in Angel's wet pussy, she cries out again, "Brian! Please! Please!" He pushes so gently inside of her as she screams out again. He kisses her, and he begins to push deeper. Angel holds onto the leg of the couch, but Brian grabs her hand, he interlocks his fingers in hers. He wanted her to feel all of him. Angel is breathing hard as Brian leans over her and begins to take her breath away; just like the first time he had erased all the hurt, she ever felt he was sucking out the pain, the hurt, and most of all, he was filling her with his love. She is overjoyed with the overwhelming sensation that Brian is giving her that she cums even harder. She squirts everywhere, the tears flow, she is shaking. Brian is not letting up. He is pushing his hard dick inside of her deeper and deeper. He is moaning with the pleasure he is feeling, he leans down and whispers in Angel's ear, "I love you. We are going to be together forever as he unloads his biggest load ever inside of Angel's wet pussy. He lays there on top of her, making sure she gets it all. Angel was truly amazed because most of the time Brian likes to pull out and let his cum fall on her, so she could see it. That night was truly amazing; it still gave Angel goosebumps.

The next day Brian had to set up commercial shoots for his gym (Push and Power Conditioning gym). Brian has

always been very proactive when it came to his business, he did a lot for his business and for the community. Brian believed in giving back. Brian worked with the local schools and also with the community sports organization. He really loved being a role model and helping young kids reach their dreams. Brian would help raise money for charity foundations to help parents who couldn't afford to have their children in camp. He is a great father, he would move mountains for them. Angel would watch Brian work hard, but he would always make time for his children; even when he was tired, he would still get up and go. He had such a good heart. That is what kept Angel loving him.

Around Father's Day, Angel recalls that Brian was down, he had shut himself off again. She worried about him because he was in the bed when she called, it seemed like he had been crying. She was very concerned. This is the second time that she knew he was in the bed feeling down. She asked him what was wrong, of course, he said he was fine. Angel always tried to make things easier for Brian. She tried to keep him motivated because she realized that trying to run a business and take care of his children were very hard for him. So, she got a plaque made for him for Father's Day. She wanted to surprise him when he came down to visit his son. She just figured he was going to come and see her as well since he was down there. But he came down but never called her or texted; he just blew her off. Angel and Jeff, Brian's son, had gotten close, so he told her that his dad came down. Angel was heartbroken; she wondered why he did not call her or come to see her. Of course, when she talked to him, he did not even let her know he came down. She wonders about that, but when things did not sit right with Angel, she speaks on it. So, Angel ended up mailing Brian's plaque off to him. Brian was so surprised. He loved it, he hung it up in the gym. Angel joked with him about how she was planning on surprising him, but he never came down. Brian was quiet then Angel said, "How come you did not tell me you came down?" Brian replied, "Oh, I was so tired. Didn't Jeff tell you how many games of basketball we played. I was going to come back, but I was tired. Angel just accepted Brian's excuse and let it go. She didn't like to argue. Time was fading between Angel and Brian. Brian seemed to not have time like he used to. The phone calls started fading down and him texting her happy whatever day it was because he didn't like to say good morning. It is now August, and the twin's birthday is on the 5th, they are planning a big party, but Brian never lets Angel come nor does he ever have her really around the twins. Angel felt like Brian kept her in this bubble away from that side of the tracks, so she felt like an outsider she felt like Brian was hiding something from her.

While Brian is working on the commercial, Angel decides to go to the gym to leave Brian to do all his business; she did not want to get in the way, with all that planning and stuff. Brian was so excited that he immediately got on the phone to make sure that his assistant had everything set up. Angel grabbed her bag and headed out. "Love you, babe!" Brian yelled, "Love you, too." Angel loved working out, it helped her to relax, and it kept her in shape. She was very particular on how she wanted her body to look and to make sure her body stayed right to keep Brian's eye. While at the gym, Angel's mind is everywhere, she just can't believe that her and Brian are still together considering everything. Angel gets on the treadmill, and her mind is just going back to that call.

August the 14th, Angel's doctor calls. She is home from work just laying around in bed, wondering why Brian has been so distant and what happened to them. He used to brag about her to his friends about how beautiful and sexy she is. He had told Angel that one day one of his female friends had called him. She was questioning him about this ex-guy friend who she had recently hooked back up with. The lady asked Brian why the man she was seeing did not respond back to a picture she sent him. The lady said he must be gay. Brian was upset with that remark, he gave her his logical opinion. He asked her how long were you two together before and how much did you weigh back then? Brian was very big on weight. He always told Angel the only way he would leave her if she got fat. He didn't care for big women; he was very clear about that. The lady responded with 7 years and that she had gained like 50+ pounds. Brian told her, "If he didn't want you back then, what makes you think he would want you now? It doesn't mean he is gay; he may not be attracted to you. He began to tell her about Angel and how they were going on a cruise. Angel has been planning this cruise forever; that is her only dream to finally take a cruise with her King. Brian told the lady that when Angel and he get on the beach, everyone is going to be looking at them, that even then he would always touch Angel because he can't stop touching her. He told her if he were to show her a picture of Angel's body that she would swear she was about 30 years old because she stays fit and takes pride in her body. Angel smiled on the inside to hear Brian tell her that story. That made her feel so good and special to know he saw her like that.

Angel wanted those days back, but they were fading away because time was no more. Brian was so distant, he barely called anymore; Angel tried so hard to reach out to him. Brian would have an answer to why he could not call, but to Angel, it never made sense, and it really hurt her. She really wanted to believe what Brian had told her, that they would be together forever. Angel hears her doctor say, "Are you alone?" Angel replies, "Yes." "Are you sitting down?" Dr. Kim asked. Angel can feel the air leave her body, and her stomach started rumbling. She could feel her anxiety start to kick in, she is thinking not cancer again. Angel was so scared her emotions were everywhere. Just then she hears her doctor say, "HIV, you have HIV." Angel was like, "What? What are you for real? What? No, this cannot be... NO!" Dr Kim told Angel she had to run another test to make sure. Angel was devastated as she fell to the floor. The tears were coming, she felt numb, sick to her stomach. She hung up the phone. All she remembers hearing was: "HIV. You have HIV." It just kept ringing in her ear. Angel just kept getting sick to her stomach. She was in shock. "No, this cannot be real. How did this happen? No, God, no!"

CHAPTER 3:

LOSING YOURSELF

Angel sits on the bed, crying, still in shock, thinking how this could be. "Once again, God, you punished me/ Why? I just wanted to be loved." Just then Angel felt that little girl come back as she balls up into a fetal position in deep thought. She picks up the phone and calls Brian. She is crying, Brian is trying to understand what she is saying, "What? What is it baby? What is wrong?" Brian was at the gym working out, Angel tells him that she now understands why he has been so distant; she tells him that he needs to go get checked that someone gave him something, Brian is still asking what is wrong. She tells him she has HIV, that he gave her HIV. Brian said, "What? No, baby. I am on my way." He immediately comes over; he tells her to leave the door open. Angel is in the bed, crying, while Brian is sitting at her side. He grabs her and holds her real tight. He tells her he didn't know; he didn't know. He said, "How can this be? He just finally found the right one and now this. How? Angel is just crying, not sure on what to feel. She feels herself fading away to that dark place that little girl used to go when she would hurt. Brian only stayed for probably 20 minutes because Angel's next to the oldest son Timothy had stopped over. She had to pull herself together, so he wouldn't know that anything was wrong. Brian left but later called her, said he had a breakdown. Angel really didn't care, nor did she believe him; she was just still in shock and upset that he could just leave her like this, empty with nothing but thoughts. She worried about everything: is she going to die? How does this work? Oh my God," she cried, "I have HIV!" She just couldn't believe it. What do I do? She started doing research, looking up how long she has to live. She found out that there is medicine you have to take; you take it every day for the rest of your life. Angel found out that there are a lot of people with HIV that gave her a little hope but still she was ashamed and very much embarrassed. Her of all people, how could this be. She felt she did everything right except for protection and falling in love. Angel just then thought back to that amazing night that Brian took her out to Andretti's, how he had made passionate love to her, told her they would be together forever. She started to get sick to her stomach. *Did he do this to me on purpose?* she thought, *to make sure she would always be his*. She cried even harder. She couldn't or didn't want to believe it, but she felt he did. Her heart just sank, she just cried and cried till she made herself sick. She was throwing up; she had the shits. She couldn't believe it. Why?

Angel is running on the treadmill, trying to fight back the tears, remembering that day she lost herself to her sickness, to the separation, to the hurt, to the pain. Angel was hurting from remembering how she had to endure going through this all by herself. It made Angel angry because she remembers how much Brian didn't care, how he never called or tried to make an appointment with her. Angel just ran till she could feel herself get weak; she knew she had to try to think of something else. She had to get back to reality. Her happy place.

Angel thinks back to the first time he came over and spent the night with her. It was Saturday night May 12; Brian had arrived around 10:30-ish. He was in sweatpants, he needed to take a shower. Angel did not think anything of it, just was happy he was there and staying the night with her. Brian took his shower, came to bed; Brian sleeps naked while Angel has on everything from her bra, tank top, panties, and shorts. Brian was like, "Are you going to take anything off? Angel was still kind of shy with her body; that little girl in her wanted to just jump under the covers and hide. She took a deep breath, she started to take everything off. Angel jumped in the bed and pulled the covers over her. Brian laughed and moved over to her. He held her; Angel could feel Brian's dick begin to grow as he was spooning her. She felt his dick getting harder and harder. He was caressing and rubbing her breast. Angel was shaking and moaning, she could feel her pussy get wet. She was so excited. Brian had begun to tease her as he took his fingers and began to play with her wet pussy, getting it even wetter. He opens her legs up, goes down between them, begins to lick her pussy. Angel feels herself floating away. She is breathing heavy as she releases all the fluids, she had in her into his mouth. Brian is enjoying himself; he continues to lick her he goes deeper. Angel starts to speak, but it was nothing she or him could understand. It was like she was speaking in tongues. She grabs Brian's head, tells him to stop, she calls him the devil. Brian laughs but he keeps going. Angel tries to move away, but Brian grabs her and continues. Angel is so weak she is breathing heavy she feels herself getting lightheaded. She tells Brian, "Please, please stop. I am going to pass out." Brian kept going. Angel is no more. She is gone with the clouds, floating in peace as she had passed out. Brian kisses Angel on her lips and whispers, "Do you love me?" Angel couldn't speak. She never really looked at Brian's dick until now, and it was big. She was wondering how in the hell was he getting that in her. Brian tells Angel to breathe as they both exchange their spirits into each other. Angel can feel herself fading away with every breath Brian took. Brian puts his big dick in Angel's wet pussy. Angel lets out a cry. No, no but she loved every bit of the hurt; it pleased her. Brian kisses her lips and whispers again, "Do you love me?" this time Angel replied, "Yes, yes." Brian is now inside of her pussy; he is giving all that Angel can handle with every stroke. Angel feels herself falling into a deep sleep as she continues to speak in a language that only the heavens can read. Angel is lost in the pleasure that she has never experienced with a man. Her body is shaking. Brian is pushing and pumping harder. He tells her to say his name. Angel says, "Yes, Brian! Yes, Brian!" Brian was so excited by how tight Angel's pussy is that he called out, "Is this my tight pussy?" Angel said yes, Brian goes deeper and begins to go faster and harder. Angel can barely take it; she feels her legs shaking as she squirts everywhere. She is losing herself, she feels herself fading again. She tells Brian, "Oh no, I am going to pass out. Stop!" Brian is in his own galaxy now. He is moving to the beat of the music of the moistness that is flowing from Angel's pussy. He is lost in the flow of the river that is flowing down his dick that he continues to push and just as he can no longer take it, he pulls his dick out and releases all the cum he had built up onto Angel's stomach. Angel is off the bed and is laying on the floor now. Brian gets up and kisses her He laughs but picks her up and places her in the bed.

The morning comes which is Mother's Day, Angel had no idea that what took place last night was going to happen again in the morning. Brian made love to Angel again in the morning. She couldn't believe it again. She could barely handle last night. She hasn't even recuperated from last night; she was still half asleep. Angel enjoyed every minute of Brian and she loved every inch of his body. He was so sexy to her. He made love to her, kissed her, he laughed and said Happy Mother's Day. Angel laughed too, she was like, "Oh yes, a very happy one." Brian left, and Angel went back to sleep. Angel slept until 3:00 p.m. She was awakened by Brian's phone call checking up on her. Brian was happy to hear she was still in bed. Angel lost herself that day.

Angel is heading home now. Her emotions are everywhere, she knows that she has to keep the good memories of how Brian makes her feel, so she won't let the past take her back to those awful places where she loses herself to the wonder of why? The how come and

the not enough. Angel just wanted to feel the love that grows when she hears Brian's voice and when she is in his arms. To see him smile when he looks at her.

Angel is left with a lot of whys; Brian would give her this feeling that he is hiding something. Brian would keep his phone face down a lot, he would never ask her to come over his house. Brian would just show up to Angel's house. Angel remembers the first time Brian came over in the daytime. It was around 4:00 in the afternoon, she was coming from her sister's house. He had called her and asked where she was. She told him she was on her way home. Angel didn't know he was sitting in her driveway. She pulled up. She was listening to her gospel music, getting filled. She was so busy worshipping that she didn't even notice that she had parked right next to him. She got out her truck, he jumped out. She was so happy to see him, he had flowers. Her heart was overjoyed. She knew then that she must just be overthinking about him hiding stuff. Angel felt he loved her, and they enjoyed that day. Brian sat with her, they went to the movies and had dinner. He spoiled her that day.

Angel pulls up to the house. Brian is in the house, laying on the couch. He says, "Hey love, you had a good workout?" Angel smiles because she remembers going

over Brian's house for the first time. And him always on the couch. "Yes, love, I did. Did you get everything in order for the commercial tomorrow? Yes, it is going to be lit." "I can't wait to see it." Angel headed upstairs to take her a nice hot bubble bath. She just wanted to soak her muscles and just clear her head. She really just wanted to get away from Brian because she didn't want him to feel her energy.

Brian had asked Angel to come over to his house. Angel was very excited to finally see where Brian had lived. She arrived at his house. Brian said the door was open and to just come in. Angel came in, Brian was laying on the couch. Brian got up, hugged her, and began to show her his house; he was very proud of it. He had wanted to do a lot to it. Brian's backyard was huge. That was his favorite thing about the house. Brian had a lot of dreams for his house and goals that he was trying to meet, and he wanted to be successful. He wanted to have everything and to be able to take care of his family. He was tired of struggling and asking for help. Angel admired that in him. He worked hard; at least he led her to believe that. Angel did not stay long. She and Brian cuddled on the couch for a couple of hours. Angel just watched Brian sleep really. Angel just wondered what Brian thought about when he was alone or when he had down time to himself. Brian always seems so distant at times Angel thought, but right now while he is laying on her lap he is at peace. Brian wakes up and kisses Angel he asked her if she was okay. "Yes, I am fine." "I know that," Brian said. Angel smiles and gets up to leave. "Love you, babe." Brian hugs her and kisses her goodbye. "Love you too, love," Angel says, and she headed back home.

Angel heads up stairs to get her bath ready; she just wanted to cry in the tub from losing herself to the past pain and hurt that Brian caused her. He never really understood or knew how much hurt he caused Angel back then. It was like things got worse. Angel lost more and more of herself because she held onto memories, that she still from this day don't know what Brian felt back then, but she knew he loved her, but she doubts it because of his actions; it was so difficult for her that he made her lose herself to the why? How come? And what now? As Angel lays in the tub, thoughts just keep coming in her head, and she can feel the tears begin to fall.

By now Brian had really become distant after Angel found out about the HIV. At first Brian was supportive; he was asking her how she was and told her he would go with her to her appointment one day. He was trying all these herbal remedies he found on YouTube, he even brought stuff for Angel to try but he wanted to try it out first to make sure it was safe. Angel knew when he said one day that it meant never. He always would promise her things, and when he said one day, it never happened. She kept asking him to go on vacation with her on a cruise or to the cabins. He would say "we will see" or "one day" or "let me check my schedule" which he would never get back to her about. Angel would cry, but she just could not understand why he acted like he did not want to spend time with her. Was she boring? Was she really that bad? Nothing made sense. Brian once could not wait to get to her. He said she was his peace, and she loved that. Angel had lost herself to this disease, and it made her doubt her self-worth. She didn't feel attractive anymore. She was calling Brian every day for him to reassure her, but instead she got short answers, sometimes no answers. She was blowing up his phone because she was afraid of losing him. She didn't know what she would do without him. Who would want her? How would she be able to date? The fear overtook her; she was alone trying to find her way. Brian didn't understand, he was moving farther and farther away. Angel would call him, trying to get him to make her feel special, to get confirmation that he still wanted and needed her. But Brian couldn't because he was battling his own demons. Angel remembers when one night she was asking Brian how come he didn't ask her to come over his house. Brian was complaining about how tired he was after work, Angel said, "Well, I can come to you sometimes." So, Brian gave in, and he told her she could come. Angel really needed to see Brian, to have him hold her, to just be next to him, so she could sleep. It's 10:30 p.m. Angel gathers all the stuff she needed for work, and she drove out there to Brian. He was already in the bed. Angel got changed, lay down beside Brian. Brian was having a hard time sleeping, so he took some sleeping pills, and for the first time Brian started opening up to Angel. Brian began to share some of his secrets. Brian began to tell Angel that when he was young, he was so poor that it was very hard for him. He remembers being in a shack like house that only had one room in it. He and his brother and mother and father stayed there. Brian said that he remembers having to take a bucket and defecate in it then take it out to dump it. He barely had food at times, they moved around a lot. Brian said his father was in jail, and later his brother ended up in jail too. Brian said his father was selling crack and other drugs. His mother, he believed when his dad was in jail, was selling herself to provide food and stuff for them. Brian said he later grew up selling drugs as well just to make it. Brian told Angel that he then became a male stripper, he was then able to afford things he wanted. Brian wasn't proud of being a stripper. He told Angel to please never talk about that or bring it up. It was hard for him. Angel agreed as Brian went on. Angel just knew there was more Brian was not sharing with her, but she just listens. Brian had told Angel he loved everything about her, but he just didn't like how her daughter would speak to her at times. Angel agreed. Brian asked Angel if she had any questions, she wanted to ask that she needed to ask them now while he had the medicine in him. Those sleeping pills were like truth serum to him. Angel asked about what happened with him and his ex-wife. Brian said it was both their fault that he just couldn't be with her because she made him feel less than a man. Brian and Angel later fell asleep. Brian held Angel in his arms. Angel was happy because that was just what she needed, just to be in his arms. Morning came, and when Brian arose, he woke Angel up with a kiss. They both got dressed. While Angel was getting dressed, Brian had gone out and started up Angel's truck, so it would be nice and warm for her. Angel thought, *Man, I could get used to this every morning*. Angel dreamed of the day of becoming Mrs. Ward. She wonders though if he would keep his word.

Angel gets out the tub, she dries herself off; she is feeling a little better. Angel started thinking about when she went to meet Brian's family, how Brian really didn't want her to go, but Angel really didn't give him a choice. Angel was determined to get Brian to share that side of town with her because she wanted to see and know everything about him since they were going to be married. Brian was trying not to share that side with her.

It was now in November. Angel and Brian had been dating a year now. Angel had planned a nice getaway for them to go on a cruise in November. It was going to be a 5-day cruise to celebrate Brian's birthday and their 1-year anniversary. Angel was so excited to finally have Brian all to herself, to finally be able to have her dream come true. Angel was always the third wheel on the cruises she would take with her sister-in-law and brother. She hated it; she had fun but just dreamed of one day cruising with a man she loved to have that experience was something so dreamed of. Angel was getting everything ready. Angel remembers when she asked Brian if he could get away, she was ready for him to say, "let me check my calendar" or "we will see", but to her surprise Brian had said to make it happen. Angel was on cloud nine. She got all the final touches; she was counting down the days. Brian had called

Angel one night and told her his dad was in the hospital. Brian really did not have a strong relationship with his father. His mother had told him one day when he drove down to see her that he needs to go talk to his dad. Brian could not understand why his mother of all people would tell him to go talk to his dad when he left her and is now married to a woman Brian really does not care for. Brian obeys and drives to go talk with his dad, later to find out that his dad had prostate cancer, and it was not looking good.

Brian sat at the hospital with his dad for hours, but they never really shared much. Brian held in a lot when it came to his feelings, he wore a mask just like Angel did to protect that little boy in him. Brian would call Angel when he was leaving the hospital. Angel can tell it did not sound good. She asked Brian if he was going to be okay, Brian said yes. Angel wondered if she should try to change the date for the cruise, but Brian said that everything should be okay. Everything was not okay. Brian's dad ended up dying a couple days later. Brian had just left the hospital from seeing him and got the call that his dad had passed away. Brian was hurt, but he did not show how bad he was hurt; he hid it. He called Angel, and he told her the news Angel could feel his grief through the phone. She could tell he was holding back his tears. Angel wanted Brian to come to her so she could hold him and comfort him. Brian just wanted to be alone, Angel hated that he shut her out. Angel didn't really know what to do because the cruise was set. It was three days away, but she worried because of the funeral services. She was hoping they had it on Wednesday or Thursday, not Friday, which was the day they were supposed to leave. Brian called her on Wednesday, asked what day they are supposed to leave, and Angel told him Friday. He was talking with his dad's wife to see if she was going to have the funeral on Thursday. Well, the days go by, and Brian is upset, hurting, he is just trying to please everybody. His dad's wife has decided to have the funeral on Friday. Brian had said he was not going. Angel knew it was going to happen like this; she could never catch a break. That little girl in her starting to cry, "Why God? Why do you keep doing this? Angel was kind of happy Brian was not going to go, but she knew it was selfish of her to feel like that. Brian later called her and told her that his dad's sister wanted him there, and he told her okay. Brian asked if Angel could change the date or something. Angel said that it was too late that she had already tried. Angel did not pay the extra fee for the insurance, so they were out of luck. Angel was so hurt, so she just cried, she blamed Brian like somehow, she felt he didn't really want to go, so she got mad. She just didn't want to understand, but she knew she had to. She just wanted to be selfish for once, so they hung up the phone. The next day she called him to apologize, she told him she was spoiled, she was being selfish, the last thing you needed is for me putting more pressure on you. Angel told Brian she loved him and she was here for him, and she asked Brian to forgive her. Brian told her he loved her.

Brian had called Angel and told her he needed a favor to ask of her, but he would call her later. Angel wondered what that could be, she wandered all day and waited for Brian to call her back. Brian did not call until the next day. He asked Angel if she was coming to the funeral. Angel didn't know what to say because she had spent all that money on the cruise, she couldn't get her money back, but she wondered why he didn't ask her sooner, she could have probably got someone to take her place. He just now asked her the day of the funeral. She said that she did not plan on it because he didn't ask her or let her know. Brian thought she was going because he had told his son Jeff that Angel was going to bring him down, so he would not have to drive out that way. Angel told Brian, "I can still bring Jeff down there to you." Brian was happy to hear that. Angel was kind of sad because she felt Brian really did not want her to go; he just needed her to bring his son down. Angel did not mind. She loved Jeff; she always enjoyed their time together. Angel remembers the first time she took Jeff grocery shopping once he had gotten settled in on campus. They laughed and talked a lot. He was so helpful and patient. Surely Angel thought he didn't get that from his dad. She laughed at the thought. When Brian had called her, she told him that Jeff is helping her find stuff and likes shopping with her. Brian said to tell Jeff to back off now. They all laughed.

Angel arrives at Brian's place; she drops Jeff off; Angel goes in later because she was a little upset because there was a misunderstanding between Jeff and his dad. Jeff had told Angel that his dad was not going to be at the house because he was picking up the twins, but Brian had told her he was not bringing the twins to the funeral. Angel was upset because she wanted to see Brian to make sure he was ok. Brian had just passed them as they had turned in his complex, but Jeff had wanted something to eat, so Angel took him to get something to eat. Angel figured why not? It did not matter Brian had left. Angel finally goes in, and to her surprise, Brian was inside. She was so happy. Brian ran up to her, hugged and kissed her, he looked at her like he had just fallen in love all over again. Angel knew she did. Her heart was racing with excitement. Brian, of course, made a joke and told Angel, "Damn, baby, you look good. Let's go upstairs." Angel was all ready to go because it has truly been a while since she and Brian had made love. Brian started laughing as Angel turned to go upstairs. He said, "No baby, I was joking. The kids are here." Just then, little James came peeking around the corner. Angel thought he was so cute, she grabbed him, took him over to the couch with his sister. Angel played with them until it was time for them all to leave. Brian walked her out to her truck, he asked her if she was okay. Brian could always feel Angel, she could never understand how he did that. He was so connected to her that he felt when she was uneasy. Angel said, "I thought you weren't going to be at the house. Jeff told me you had already left." Brian gave his famous smirk and said, "I knew it was something." He grabbed her and kissed Angel, told her he loved her, and she left.

Angel went on her cruise by herself with her sister and her male friend. Angel felt so alone, she missed Brian so much. Angel called Brian on this app on her phone, so they were able to video chat. Angel really did not know how to use the video, Brian had to coach her. Angel was just happy to see him, to see that he was doing okay. They talked every chance they got. Angel felt good to see Brian and to hear his voice. She was able to enjoy herself a little, but she still wanted Brian there. Brian told Angel he missed her. She loved hearing that. Angel tried really hard to enjoy herself. Her sister and her man were having a little issue. Angel just pretty much stayed in her room thinking about Brian. Angel returns home, and Brian could not wait to have her in his arms. He came over, and they spent the night together in each other's arms. It really felt good, Angel thought, to finally have Brian anxious and missing her. Thanksgiving was just around the corner. Angel wondered if Brian was going to invite her to meet the family. Brian had come over on the 23rd. They were watching the football game; both their teams were playing against each other. Angel loved just how comfortable Brian would be when he came over. He just lay around like this was his house. Angel loved that because she wanted him to feel peace and at home with her. Angel's team is the Pittsburgh Steelers, and Brian's are the Patriots. While Brian was lying on the couch, he was on the phone talking about Thanksgiving plans to a family member. Angel was like, okay this is her chance, so she asked Brian what are you doing for Thanksgiving, he told her he was going home. Brian asked her what she was doing, she said going with you. Brian laughed and proceeded to try to avoid the conversation, but Angel did not let him this time. Angel told Brian, "You never take me home. Why? This is the perfect time for you to take me." Brian really could not say anything, so he finally gave in and told her she can come with him.

It was Thanksgiving Day. Angel had just got out of the shower getting dressed. Brian video called her. Angel forgot she was naked and answered the phone. Brian laughed and said, "Damn, baby, cover up." Thank God it was me calling you not someone else, with you being naked I would beat your ass. Angel said sorry as she blushed. Brian was making small talk, and then he got to the point he was trying to make an excuse for Angel not to go. He told her that he did not think his mom would have time to really sit down and talk to her. He did not want Angel to feel out of place or that his mom was being rude because he really wanted them to get along. Brian told her that he did not want her to get mad if his mother was distant because of all the family members. Angel told him it was not going to be a problem; she would be fine. Angel could see the look on his face as he continued to try to talk her out of coming. Angel was getting upset. "If you do not want me to go, then just say so," Angel told him. Brian reassured her that was not the case; he wanted everything to be perfect. He was just nervous is all. Angel told him, "It will be okay. I just want to see where you live and spend a holiday with you at least meet the family too." Brian said. "Okay baby, hurry up." They hang up. Angel continues to get dressed. She puts on this nice button up dress with purple heels. She packed some sandals just in case her feet started to hurt. She walked out the house and headed to Brian's house. Brian greets her at the door. He is outside cleaning his truck out, but he was not sure if he wanted to drive his truck because he got in an accident; his truck had front end damage. Angel did not care about that, but Brian said she was too classy. He did not want her riding in his damaged truck. So, they took Angel's BMW. On the way down, they small talk about how far out he lives, and he told her that there is not much out there. Brian asked if she brought some other shoes. Angel said yes, he said okay because they will be outside. Angel thought that it's going to be cold later. Brian then kind of let Angel know she was a little overdressed, so they stop at the closest Walmart. Brian buys Angel some sweatpants and a shirt; Angel needed a bra, too, because she had a lace set underneath the dress. Brian would not buy her one because he did not like for her to wear Walmart bras. Angel didn't buy Walmart bras either; she has only worn Victoria Secret bras. Brian liked for her panties and bras to match always. Angel changed her clothes in the truck. She felt so awkward because she did not have a bra on. It bothered her, but Brian said she looked fine. Angel was getting nervous as they got closer to Brian's hometown. They pull up into a carwash, so Brian could wash off Angel's truck. Angel just watched him as she videos him, loving every moment of being spoiled by him. Brian drove Angel around; he showed her the shack he stayed in when he was young. Angel couldn't believe it. They drove all around as Brian told his stories of his childhood, he showed her all the local spots he hung out at. Angel said, "Wow, this is out in the country." Brian was not lying; there was not much out here. They finally make it to Brian's brother's place. He stayed in a double wide trailer. Angel could feel her heart racing as she exited the truck. She felt like she looked a hot mess. She was so upset with Brian for not telling her ahead of time about being outside and what to wear. She approaches the trailer, and there were two elder women sitting out on the porch. Brian introduces his mom Karen and her sister Tracey. Angel takes a deep breath and says hello trying to get past how underdressed she was. She wished she just kept on the dress. Brian had introduced her to just about everyone including his brother and his wife. It all seems to be going fine Angel thought, until the mother's sister,

Tracey, came up to Angel and said, "Aren't your feet cold?" Angel had her sandals on. Angel was like no, she said, "Girl, it is too cold for you to have your feet out like that." She went on and on about it. Angel just wanted to tell her to shut up, but she explained to her what had taken place, that she had to change because she didn't know that she was going to be out in the woods. Angel was getting pissed because really, she wanted to make a good impression and she felt like she failed, and she looked like shit.

The food was done, and everyone gathered around in a circle or as close as they could. Angel had no idea what was going to take place. Suddenly they started going around the circle, and everyone would tell what they were thankful for. Angel loved stuff like that; she was such a romantic and feeling person. They got to this one guy who it seems like he does the same thing every year. Angel could tell just from everyone's facial expression. He said a prayer and began to sing. Angel loves music especially when it's about God. Everyone joined in, Angel did as well. It was so powerful to Angel that it moved her. Brian wasn't feeling it. Angel laughed because she figured it's because Brian couldn't hold a note to save his life. Brian made fun of Angel when she would sing all the time. He loved her voice but didn't like her to sing. Angel thought that made no sense. It came time for Brian to say what he was thankful for, he said he was thankful for family and for having Angel there with him. Angel felt so special. Angel was so nervous. She said she was thankful to be able to meet them all and to be able to share this amazing experience and for having Brian in her life. It was so nice. They went to meet other family members, they stopped at his stepmom's house to check on her. Angel was so happy he brought her. They headed back home. Brian had to stop at the twin's moms to drop off some medicine since the twins were sick, so Angel drove home, Brian came over later.

Angel is lying in the bed now, just thinking back to that day. Brian comes upstairs and lays next to her. Angel hasn't put on any clothes yet. Brian says, "Babe, what's wrong?" Angel said, "Nothing is wrong," but Brian said, "You know I know you, and I can feel you. So, tell me what is on your mind." Angel loved and hated that about Brian, how he felt her. Angel told him she was just thinking about their life and how happy she is now. Brian reached over, gave her a kiss, and said, "Good, because I love making you happy, and I plan on doing that forever." Brian then proceeded to touch Angel's body, and they made love. Angel loses herself in the thought of everlasting peace.

CHAPTER 4:

Loving in the Midst of the Storm

The first time Angel and Brian argued or had a disagreement, it was over Valentine's Day. Brian was so not feeling that day. Angel told Brian when they first met that there were only two days special to her, and those were Valentine's Day and her birthday. Brian agreed that he would make those days special for her. So now it is the day before Valentine's Day, and Brian hadn't said a word. Angel was hoping that Brian was going to surprise her. So, all day at work, she tried to stay positive. Brian never called or said a word to Angel. Angel knew she felt it in her gut that he was not going to do anything, but she tried to stay positive. Well, it's Valentine's Day and still nothing from Brian, not a call, not nothing. Angel was sad and hurt, she felt like she didn't ask for much, just anything from Brian a note or something would have made her day. Angel remembered when Brian first wrote her a letter; it was the best. They had just started dating, he was supposed to come over and take her to lunch. Brian had gotten her times mixed up when she was to report to work that Angel waited and no Brian, so she left. The day went on, and Brian called her. He asked her how she was doing, she said fine and that she was at work. Brian said, "I thought you got off at 6:00pm?" She said, "No, I start at 6:00 p.m." Brian was so mad that he got the times messed up, that he came to her job and had dinner with her. He gave her a letter he had written, he told her to read it when he was gone. Brian's letter really shocked her she couldn't believe he had written her a letter. She felt so special, Brian had written that he was so happy she was in his life, that he couldn't let this day go by without telling her how special she is, how blessed he is to have found someone like her. He said he loved her; Angel was so touched. But Brian did nothing for Valentine's Day, so Angel went home from work upset and hurt. Brian called her later, she asked him why he didn't do anything for her. Brian gave a sorry excuse about it just being an unnecessary holiday and not important and how stupid it is. Angel was hurt, she said, "It's not stupid to me, and it matters to me." Angel said, "I told you how special it was to me, and you said 'ok,' you would make sure you will do that." Brian went on and was really upset. He yelled at Angel and said, "It's just a fucking day!" Angel said, "But you promised me you would not forget it and you were okay with it." The conversation got so heated that Brian told Angel to get off his line. Angel was like, "I'm not on your line," she didn't know what that meant, so she said, "Brian really? Really, you're going to hang up on me?" Brian never hung up, but nothing was solved; they just said goodbye, Angel cried herself to sleep. Brian didn't know the value of that day. It was the only day she could have; it was just special to her. Later in the night, Brian called, he told her he was sorry for yelling at her and asked her if she still loved him. "Yes, Brian I still love you." But Angel was hurt still.

It was Angel's birthday now, and she was still hurt over Valentine's Day. She didn't really expect anything from Brian, so she just went through the day empty. She got home, showered, and got ready for bed. Angel heard a knock at the door. It was Brian. He had balloons and a gift with a card. Angel was so excited; she couldn't believe it. She ran and jumped in his arms. Angel opened her card; it was the best card ever. She was so happy to see he still loved her so much. Angel opened her gift. It was a necklace with a key. Brian said she was the key to his heart. Angel just jumped in his arms again. Angel loved Brian so much, she couldn't imagine not having him in her life that it scared her because they had just started dating. Brian was so positive and very sure on how he felt about her that he told her he knew she was the one from day one because the universe told him. Angel was so amazed by Brian's positive energy, she just felt she could really learn a lot from him. Brian had such strong faith, he just seemed like he never worried about anything at least he didn't in the beginning.

Angel was just lying there after making love to Brian, saying, "Damn, now, I got to take another shower," but it was well worth it. She got back in the shower. Brian had headed out to go workout. Brian needs his time alone so he could just refuel himself, he gets overwhelmed at times with dealing with people on a daily basis. Brian loves his alone time, and Angel doesn't mind because he is always at peace when he comes back. He just seems like he appreciates her more, she knows that Brian needs to just release all of the negative energy that comes with running his business. He knows at times he can be an asshole, so he tries not to bring that stuff home to Angel.

Time is going by since Angel felt Brian, he had made himself very distant. She would see him once a month, and then it turned into once in two months. After Brian's dad died and the HIV thing, Brian was hardly reachable. He would ignore some of Angel's texts and phone calls. He would have excuses on why he couldn't come over to see her. Angel was so lonely and hurt, she didn't know what to do because she didn't know what was going on. When she did talk to Brian, he would just blow it off and say he still loves her. Angel was trying to hold onto that love, that feeling that they had back then. She was hurting and felt empty. She was trying to be strong, but she was empty from the poison growing inside of her. Angel remembers her first doctor's appointment and how she was so embarrassed about her having HIV. What would her peers think? What would her children think? It was driving Angel crazy, she just would sink more into that unwanted depression, but she was so good at hiding her feelings. Angel pushed through the days and the months of not really seeing Brian or even talking to him.

Brian finally came over. It was June 8th when he finally came over to see Angel. She was so happy but also sad because she was hurt, she knew if she expressed her feelings, it would spoil the mood. Angel wanted everything to be perfect. She made dinner for him. She even put on something sexy, something she really doesn't do, but she just wanted Brian to look at her the way he used to. She wanted him to just be happy with just being in her presence. Brian comes in and sees Angel; he couldn't keep his hands off her. Angel loved that about him. He was very affectionate. They ate dinner, but Angel just felt something was wrong. Something just wasn't right. Even though Brian was there, he really wasn't. Angel was just hurting inside, but she hid it and went back to the room and tried to fight back the tears. She put some pants over the sexy outfit she had on since she was feeling uncomfortable. Brian didn't like that she had covered up, so he pulled the pants down and began to touch her. They went to the bedroom where they made love and went to sleep. Angel couldn't really sleep because she just couldn't shake the feeling of not knowing what was going on with Brian. They awoke in the morning and Brian kissed Angel goodbye, but he didn't look at her like he used to. It was like he was hiding something.

Angel gets up and starts dinner. She and Brian are having a movie night. Angel is going over to Elizabeth's house to pick up the twins and her youngest daughter up so they can spend time. Angel looks forward to movie night with the kids she loves the kid's movies. Angel is just a big kid so she couldn't wait to watch the new Croods movie. Brian always falls asleep, but she still loves cuddling up under him, just listening to his heartbeat. Angle had made snacks for the kids, Brian would always doze off and the kids would laugh because he would always say he is awake, but Angel knew he was asleep. She remembers their first movie night.

Brian seemed like he was coming around. He was talking to Angel more, he sent her a good morning text again. Angel had to go out of town for a week for training, so she was feeling down because of the distance between her and Brian. He would still just text every blue moon, but he didn't call her at night like he used to. She was really hurting and trying to deal with this HIV alone was killing her. Angel didn't understand why Brian didn't care or even think about how she felt. Angel thought maybe she forgave him too quickly. but that is just how she is. Angel sat in class just thinking of the last time she really spoke with Brian. She wondered why he didn't want to talk to her at night anymore since he used to say he needed to hear her voice before he went to sleep. He would fall asleep on the phone talking to her, but nothing was making sense to Angel. Her heart was hurting with all of this distance and non-communication between them. Angel remembers a poem she wrote him, trying to let him know how she was feeling.

WHERE ARE YOU

I'm walking in circles hoping to find US. Instead, when I look in the mirror

There is only myself. My heart is heavy as the night grows,

Longing, wondering when I will be in your arms.

My pillow holds the tears of my shame as

My heart continues to beat in pain.

As a day goes by and then a week I

Realize it's just only me. I'm walking

In circles dealing with the fight of

The lonely cries, hoping that you finally

Realize, I'm walking in circles holding onto

Your words that one day, one day they would be

Heard. Days becomes weeks of total peace, oh the joy of being

Able to lay together in the sheets. I'm walking

In circles holding onto your actions that poured into me

Giving us total satisfaction. You took my breath away

With just a whispered "do you love me?" was the question.

I call for you. Can you hear? I'm screaming out. Can you feel

Me near? I'm looking for Brian, what used to be US

Is now only ME....

It was so hard for Angel to sit in class, trying to hold back her tears. She was not focused on anything, but why Brian was not calling or coming to see her. The class went to lunch. Angel didn't really have an appetite, so she just went walking, and she started praying. *God, please give me a sign, not sure on which way to go. My heart is so heavy because I miss him so much. I miss when he used to call and say "Good morning, beautiful."* Angel continued to pray as the tears began to fall from her face. She was so hurt from not knowing what was going on. Angel was so upset with herself because she knew she had lost herself to this man, she didn't know how to get herself back. Having HIV made her feel like he was the only man for her. The fear kept her and her love for him kept her. It was like she was fighting two demons. Angel was overwhelmed with everything. Lunch was over, so she got herself together and sat down in class. Suddenly, her phone had vibrated. It was a text from Brian: *Good morning, beautiful.* Angel couldn't believe it. Was this a sign from God letting her know that he was the one? Angel was filled with joy, she responded: *Good morning, my love.* Brian asked how she was doing, Angel told him she was in training. She never told him that she was empty without knowing what was going on. She just kept that all in like she always does. Brian responded with: *I love you.*

Angel returns home. Brian and she are talking again. He plans to come over tonight. Angel couldn't wait; she was so excited to see him. Brian comes over, and Angel runs and jumps in his arms. Brian just gives that little smirk and tells her to get her heavy self-down. Angel holds on because she doesn't care if she falls. Brian immediately takes Angel back to the bedroom, and they make love. It was amazing. Angel thought yes, finally, her Brian is back. They slept the night away as Brian held her close. Angel was like a little kid up under Brian's arms. Angel was at peace, for the storm that was growing inside her seemed to be blowing away. Morning came, and Angel was dreading letting Brian go; she didn't want to see him leave, but Brian asked her what was for breakfast. Angel was shocked. "What? You're staying?" Angel was on cloud 9. Brian has never stayed a day with her. Brian's breakfast consists of some more of Angel. They made love again. Angel was like, Yes, *I can for sure get used to this every morning*. Brian said he was going to make breakfast, but then he changed his mind. Angel knew he wasn't going to make no damn breakfast; she knew she had him spoiled. Angel made breakfast. She made some eggs and bacon with spinach with mushrooms, and they ate. Brian took his shower first, and then Angel took hers. They decided on a movie to watch as they lay on the couch. Brian holding Angel in his arms, they decided to watch the new *Bad Boys*. Angel ordered the movie, and of course, as soon as it started, Brian was knocked out. Angel didn't care; she just enjoyed having him there this long. Brian would wake up periodically, and they would talk a little, but he would go back to sleep. It was now 4:00 p.m. Angel couldn't believe Brian stayed this long. Brian gets up and tells Angel he must go now. Brian likes to spend Sunday to himself or with the twins. It's his rest day, really where he gets most of his stuff done and just spend time with himself. He had stuff he needed to get done. Angel was okay with that; she just was happy to have finally had time, she wanted to go get in the bed and go to sleep because Brian always drains her in a good way. Angel slept with a grin on her face and just thought on how today was just a wonderful day. She hoped that Brian would keep this up and they would have movie night again.

Brian came home, and Angel had everything set up for movie night. Angle had the kids sitting at their section, Angel had set up a kid's section with their own bean bags, and trays. Brian took his shower, and they began to watch the movie. Times like this Angel loved just to sit and lay around, just spending time. Angel was always big on that. Brian would never really make the time back then. Angel never really asked for much from Brian, but time was always something Brian really never had for her. Angel is so happy that time found them both, and they are spending nothing but time. It's the little things that keep her.

After Brian had left that morning, Angel still felt like something was wrong, but she continued with her day trying to just keep the positive energy. Angel had plans to go see Mary; they were going to do lunch. Brian had sent Angel fifty dollars. Brian had seemed to get a hold of some money, so he was trying to spoil Angel. He had brought her some tennis shoes and a refrigerator for her office. Angel was looking up name plates for her desk, she sent a picture to Brian to see what he thought. He asked her how much it cost. Brian had sent her the money. Angel was happy to see that Brian loved to take care of her. It really made Angel happy, but it seemed like it really made Brian happy too. Angel never did ask Brian where the money came from. She really didn't care; she figured that Brian's business was finally paying off, she just accepted it and went on. Brian was so happy to be able to finally spoil Angel that he paid to get her feet done. Angel was on her way to Mary when a car had jumped in front of another car. The car in front of Angel stopped in mid traffic, Angel tried to stop and turn in the other lane, but there were cars coming, so Angel braced for the impact. Angel hit the vehicle in the rear, causing just a dent in its bumper. Angel's BMW was totaled. The entire front end was busted, the radiator had exploded, and there were car parts in the road. Angel was okay, nothing major, just bumps and some bruises. She was more in shock. Angel video called Brian, but he hung up on her. Then she texted him and told him she was in a car accident. Brian called immediately. Angel told him she was okay and that she was just hurt because her BMW looked to be totaled. Angel had called Timothy so he could come and pick her up. Timothy worked just around the corner. Mary was on her way as well. Angel had sent Brian a picture of the damage. He said, "Baby, I'm just glad you are okay." Timothy took Angel home and sat with her for a minute to make sure she was okay and to wait for his sister to get there. Brian had called Angel's phone, and Timothy had answered it because Angel was in the bathroom. Brian told Timothy he wouldn't know what he would have done if something had happened to Angel. They made small talk until Angel got out the bathroom. Brian was so worried; he was calling like crazy.

Angel was going to the doctors every week for her injuries. Brian was calling and checking up on her. Angel was happy to see that Brian had shown his concern. Brian even told Jeff, Karen, and his daughter Janae' about Angel's accident. He called Angel and asked if anyone had called her like his mom and the kids. She said his mom called, and that was it, but later Janae' called, and then Jeff had called. Angel knew then that she was very special to Brian.

Brian never came over to check up on Angel. She was kind of hurt by that. She thought he would have at least come over, but she just figured he must be working a lot with new clients. Time went on, and Brian stopped calling and texting again. Angel was feeling down and unwanted;

she just couldn't understand why Brian does this, why he keeps putting her off.

Brian is planning a big surprise for Angel's 55th birthday. He has it all worked out. He is finally taking her on the cruise she has been waiting for, and he wants to ask her to marry him. Brian has been struggling for a long time with all the past things he has inflicted on Angel that it still hurts him from this day. At times, it was still hard for him to look at her. The guilt would eat him up, he would think back to the day when he had given up. The guilt, the pain had consumed him to where he wanted to take his life. Brian looks at Angel now, and he just can't believe that God gave him this woman. He was so lucky to still have her. Brian wanted her to know how special she is to him.

Angel remembers when he forgot her birthday. Brian didn't call her or nothing. Angel's children came over and surprised her, they made her feel special with gifts. They all asked about Brian, but Angel kept saying he was busy she was making excuses, but Mary wasn't having it. She was really upset; said he was worthless. It hurt Angel to hear her say that, but she felt it too, but she hid her feelings behind the mask she wears as she tries to push through the day. It is now around 7:00 p.m. No word from Brian. Angel couldn't believe it. She would have never thought he would have forgotten her birthday, never. Angel thought maybe he didn't really love her; nothing was making sense. She just wanted to cry. Angel couldn't take it no more, so she called Brian, and when he answered, she said, "Did you forget something?" Brian said, "Oh, yeah. Happy birthday." Angel wanted to cuss Brian out. There was no emotion, no care in his voice; he acted like she was nothing to him. Angel always made sure she went over the top for Brian on his birthday. Angel didn't know this Brian at all; it hurt her entire soul. Angel cried herself to sleep. She just didn't care anymore. She could feel herself fading away. She hated this feeling, she hated herself for allowing herself to get so emotionally tied up in Brian till he became her air. Angel could feel the storm raging inside of her. She was just blowing away in the breeze of nothingness, not knowing what the hell was going on. Angel has lost her strength. She didn't want to fight; she wanted to give up and die. Angel didn't know how to survive in the midst of her storm. Instead of leaning on God, she was leaning on her children, and they tried to comfort her. Timothy would bring the grandchildren over, and that would work for a little bit. Timothy even tried to talk to her and help console her, but he really didn't have the patience. He had his own stuff he was dealing with. Angel tried to fight every day to not lean on her kids because sometimes it made matters worse. Angel was stuck with loving what she couldn't see or feel, but she kept believing in what used to be there. Angel didn't want to give up because to be honest she didn't know how to or was just afraid to. In the midst of the storm, Angel still loved Brian even when he did her wrong. Angel just kept giving Brian unconditional love.

CHAPTER 5:

ALONG CAME THE SUN WITH THE RAIN

Angel slept the night away with tears on her pillow. She was overwhelmed with the heartache of Brian just not even caring about her birthday. Angel started seeing a different side to Brian, she hated the way he was treating her now. She wonders what happened to her being his spoiled little princess. Angel remembers Brian telling her that he loved that about her, how spoiled she was, how he wanted to take care of her. Brian would go off on these wild ideals, he would tell her how he wanted to buy her a ring so big that it could barely fit on her finger. How he wanted to give her everything from a house to buying her a SUV just anything she wanted. Angel remembers how caring and patient Brian was. How when he had come over, she would be working on a puzzle, he would try to help her, he would try to find one piece that lasted about a minute before he gave up and spent most of his time looking at her and touching her. Angel remembers when Brian had asked her to pick out a ring. He was at his place, lying in his bed. Angel was so excited she went from picking out a ring to finding her wedding dress and planning her wedding. Angel had sent Brian a couple of rings she wanted, but Brian had one picked out. Angel remembers getting all dressed up to go visit Brian at his job. She had put on this little black dress with some black wedges. It was a short dress; it barely went to her knees. When she got there, Brian was sitting in the chair in the lobby. Angel walked in, and Brian said, "Aww, dame babe! Come here! "He grabbed Angel and proceeded to run his hands up her dress. Angel could feel herself start to get wet, Angel told Brian to stop. Brian told her it's his. Angel smiled and shook her head, but Brian had stopped and told her he didn't want her to mess up his floor. Angel pushed him away, and they both laughed. Brian had shown her the ring he had picked out for her. He told her that is just a starter ring, he planned on getting her a bigger one later. Angel really didn't care; she just was excited about the thought of getting married.

Angel awoken to a heavy heart; she still was hurt from Brian not remembering her birthday. Angel had got in the shower; she couldn't hold back tears. She hated that she cried so much. She hadn't cried this much since Peter died.

She was truly hurting, she just really wanted to stay in the bed and sleep the day away. Angel was getting dressed, she noticed her phone was ringing. It was Brian. She thought about not even answering it, giving him a taste of his own medicine, but she couldn't resist. She never could; she always gave in. Brian asked her if she was home, she said, "Yes, why?" He said, "Expect something to come to your door." Angel started to get excited. She thought Brian was going to surprise her and show up. Around 4:00 p.m., there was a knock at her door. Angel ran to open it, and to her surprise, it was a white man holding flowers. He said, "Are you Mrs. Ward?" At first Angel thought he had the wrong house, but then she realized that he meant Ward, like Brian Ward. She laughed and told the guy yes. She gets the flowers, she was so happy, but what made her even happier is what had been written on the card. He had put: To Mrs. Angel Ward, and on the inside, it read "I hope this puts a smile on your face and brings joy to your heart. I love you, and I always will love you. B. Ward." Angel was in tears of joy. She called Brian and thanked him so much because it truly made her day. Angel was like, *this is what keeps me loving him so much, he always means well, and he knows when he is wrong*. Angel was never the type to hold onto grudges, she would always forgive people if they would show that they care or apologized.

Brian had gotten everything ready for the surprise party for Angel. He had gotten all their friends over while Angel was at work. Angel had taken a short day and got off work at 8:00 pm. Angel comes home from a busy day at work. She walked in, and all these people had jumped out yelling, "Happy Birthday!" Angel was so surprised she was in tears to think Brian was planning this all this time. Brian told her to go upstairs. He had a nice hot bubble bath for her, and he had bought her a nice, sexy dress to wear. Angel ran up the stairs, she couldn't wait to get back to the party. Hell, she couldn't wait to see the dress. She thought, Fuck the bubble bath! as she almost slid down the stairs. Brian laughed. "See? That is what you get. Slow your ass down." Angel laughed and continued to run up the stairs again. Angel took her bubble bath so quick and jumped in the dress. She did her hair and makeup and headed down the stairs. This time she walked slowly and sexy, hoping Brian was down the steps waiting, so she could get his attention and make him excited.

The days go by. Everything with Brian seems to be a little better, but Angel was still not happy. He still was distant and wasn't really calling her like he used to. Angel noticed that he spent more time on social media than anything. Angel didn't understand. When he used to take his breaks, he would text her or call her. Now it was Angel who was doing all the texting and calling. Angel tried to ask Brian why he wasn't calling her or texting her like he used to. Brian would say he was busy, but Angel would say it only takes a minute to text and say I love you. She said, "You can get on social media and like a pic and write a comment, but you can't text me?" Angel was getting upset. Brian said okay. Brian tried to be a smart ass by texting Angel every two minutes sending hearts or saying he loved her. But like everything, it never lasted, but that is not what Angel had wanted anyway. She just wanted the old Brian to come back, the one who looked at her with those loving eyes.

Angel was at work one night, and a friend of hers had shown her a picture of a female who happened to be a pole dancer, she asked if she knew her. Angel told her no. Her friend had said, "You might want to look at her post because Brian is all over her page." Angel couldn't believe it. She could feel her heart racing, her stomach bubbling. She had to go to the bathroom because she was going to be sick, she had the shits. Angel sat on the toilet and pulled up the pole dancers' picture and looked at one of her pictures.

She was half naked. Hell, in just about all her pictures, she was naked, but she was a pole dancer, so that is pretty much what they wore. Angel took a deep breath and looked at the comments on what people had to say. There was Brian's picture. He had put five hearts on her picture followed by a couple of 100%. Angel couldn't believe it. She was so hurt she was crying. Once again, she was crying. "Fuck! This crying shit has to stop!" and then she noticed that he did all this on the day of her birthday. The birthday he didn't have time, nor did he remember. Angel was pissed. "He had fucking time to look at her picture and take the time he could never give me and like and heart her." Angel began to look at other pictures, and sure enough Brian was on just about all her pictures, looking thirsty. Angel was on fire because Brian did all that talk about loyalty over love bullshit. Angel was getting mad as hell. She got up from the toilet, washed her hands, and continued to look. She found some videos of Brian and the woman at his gym. They were playing around, and you can tell they were flirting. Angel was in tears now. She knew this is where her time was going. Angel didn't blame the woman. She was upset with Brian. He was the cheater and liar. Angel saw he was interacting with her; *That's not how you work as a trainer*, Angel thought. Angel continued to look and found another video of them. This time Brian was massaging her with this stick, she was barking like a dog. Like, What the fuck? Angel thought. She couldn't take it no more. She immediately called Brian and went off! Oh, Brian wasn't ready for what Angel had to say, but Brian was good. He was very quick on his toes, and he took the entire situation and blamed it on social media. Really? Angel thought. Brian said he just liked all of his client's pictures and totally got away from the hearts he had put. He turned things around so quick that Angel felt like shit for even saying anything. Angel hates arguing, she told him that was so disrespectful, and that the woman is naked. Like, she only had G-strings on and really nothing else. "Why, Brian?" Angel asked. Brian blew it off and said it meant nothing. Somehow Brian turned the entire thing around to "Angel, you need to be focused. You don't need to be doing this right now We can talk later, but baby, you need to calm down and just stay focused, and we will talk later." Angel let it go, later never came. Angel just let it go.

Brian got Angel a nice, sexy black dress. He loves black. Angel comes down, and Brian is at the steps waiting, right where Angel was hoping he would be. Brian's eyes about popped out of his head, he was getting excited. He immediately placed his hands by his crotch area to hide

the bulge that was starting to grow in his pants. Brian said, "Damn baby! Wow! I didn't know that dress was going to fit you like that." Angel had very nice breasts. Brian would always ask her if she had breast implants. Angel would always say no. Angel didn't think her breast looked that good. "Well, you picked it out, so you did good, baby." Angel smiled and just blushed. The party was going great; everyone was laughing and having a great time.

Angel finished her shift at work and went home. She was so hurt because she didn't really understand why. Angel knew Brian was lying. She felt it in her gut, but because she was so afraid of losing him, she just ignored it. She wanted to believe there was nothing really there.

Angel was crushed, her self-esteem really dropped. She found herself checking the pole dancers page and Brian was still liking everything. There were pictures of her working out, and Angel was like, Really? She worked out, and Brian would just say, "Oh, that's nice." But this woman got hearts after hearts. Angel couldn't understand. She looked so much better than her; her body was way better. Angel started slipping more and more into this competition with a woman she didn't even know. Angel did her own photo shoot and took a very sexy topless picture of herself on a workout bench, sent it to Brian and told him how she had lost her self-esteem and worth. But not no more because she knows her value. Angel was just trying to get a reaction from Brian. Brian texted back and said, "No, baby, you are beautiful." Angel didn't feel beautiful. In fact, she felt nasty and dirty. She had HIV. Who would want her? Brian didn't even want her anymore. Angel just got fed up when she saw that Brian had made a comment on one of the pole dancer's pictures. She was doing a mini photo shoot with different see-through nightgowns. Brian had put in the comments 1,2,3, and she replied then what Brian said lights out. Angel just cried because she knew then he had been sleeping with her. Picture after picture, Brian continued to stay on there. But he could never call Angel or even text her. Angel was so hurt because she was trying everything, but Brian just kept blowing her off. He would do just enough to just keep Angel satisfied.

Angel gave up. She stops looking at the pole dancer's page. She realizes it doesn't matter what she does or says to Brian; he is doing what he wants. Angel is realizing she doesn't make Brian happy anymore, so she starts sinking into a depression. She would call, text, and video call Brian all the time. It got to the point she knew Brian was ignoring her. Angel didn't care. She felt he was the blame for all her shame and her feeling unwanted. He owed her fucking TIME! He gave her this shit, and he was just carrying on like he had nothing. Angel would get pissed at times. She lost herself to anger and regret. She hated herself for being so stupid, for even going on a dating site. Angel always had this fear of catching HIV. That is why she stayed to herself. Angel knew Atlanta was high in cases, and what does she do? Fall for the first big dick man. Angel was so mad at herself, but most of all, she was mad that she lost that fight in her. She lost God along the way. She had put Brian so high that she couldn't find him. Angel remembered the sun was shining in and then came the rain with the pain. She just sat there thinking and crying, feeling sorry for herself. Angel would take these shower videos, trying to get Brian's attention, begging him. She would call begging him. Text begging him. It was crazy, but Angel was lost. She lost sight of the one and only true king she should have been begging for, who has never left her.... GOD. Angel just fell to her knees. She began to pray, and she asked God to forgive her. Angel was crying out to God to help her.

After everyone had finished eating, everyone went out to the back yard. Brian and Angel had a huge backyard with a nice pool with indigo water. They had a gazebo with a hot tub and a sauna. Brian had a guy come out and set

up fireworks to shoot off when he proposed to Angel. Brian ordered a nice cake that said Happy Birthday, Mrs. Ward. Angel was trying to figure out why they went outside since it was in the middle of February. Angel and Brian had a closed in glass balcony, so it wasn't that cold, but Angel stayed cold. Just then, Brian got down on one knee. Angel couldn't believe it. She was in tears. Brian said, "Remember when I told you forever, I know I have not always been faithful, nor did I appreciate you. I didn't value you or the time we had. I took you for granted and made you feel unwanted. I don't deserve a woman like you, but I am so happy you stuck with me. I am so happy that God gave you the patience and the heart that you have. You are a very unique woman. Sometimes when I look at you, I know God did me a big favor because I shouldn't have a woman like you. So, I am asking you, Angel, would you do me the honor of becoming my wife? Angel was in tears. Her makeup had run all down her face. Angel nodded her head and said, "Yes! Yes, Brian, I will be your wife." The fireworks went off, and the cake came in; everyone was cheering, and it was truly what Angel had been waiting on.

Angel was lost in misery and didn't know how to get out. She would call Brian, and he wouldn't answer at times, but late at night, he had no time for her. Angel just would cry herself to sleep. Every morning she would wake and try again. Sometimes Brian would be good and then nothing, but Angel kept holding on because of fear of not being able to find anyone else. She really loved Brian; she just couldn't believe this man in the first 12 months had treated her like a queen. He would run to her and loved being around her. Now he barely called her or even came to see her. Angel would just hold onto old memories on how good Brian used to be. She remembers when she was moving, she had to move her furniture. She had already made plans to have her son Timothy and her brother Ralph come over in the morning to help her. Brian had come over that night late, he wasn't in a good mood. Angel felt like he really didn't want to be there, but she tried to make everything perfect. Angel had given Brian a necklace for their 1-year anniversary. Brian would never really wear it, it bothered Angel a lot, so when Brian got in the bed, she asked him why he didn't have the necklace on. Brian told her he forgot it. Angel wouldn't let up; she kept going at him. She felt he was hiding something, and she wanted the truth. Brian just went on with lie after lie, till he got upset. Angel got mad, she tried to take off her necklace to see how he would feel. Brian was tired, he wasn't in the mood. Angel was hurt, she wasn't in the mood either, so Brain asked her if she wanted him to leave. Angel said, "I just want the truth." Brian told her to just lie down and shut her country ass up. Angel was shocked. Brian had never talked to her like that. Angel told him, "I'm not country." They both rolled over and went to sleep. Angel cried herself to sleep because she knew now the Brian she once knew was gone. Angel got no sleep really. Later in the night Brian turned over and pulled Angel close to him he held her. Angel finally fell asleep. Angel was awakened to her phone going off. It was Timothy saying he was on his way. Brian asked her who that was, she told him that Timothy was coming over to help her move. Brian then reached over and grabbed Angel. He looked at her and never spoke a word. He just kissed her and started touching her. Angel was still hurt, but she couldn't resist Brian's touch, she melted. Brian kissed Angel so softly. He began to touch her between her legs, and Angel could feel herself getting so excited. The juices from between her legs just poured out. Brian had climbed on top of her and began to slowly enter her. Angel felt her eyes start to water up. Brian looked at Angel again, and still no words came. Angel just looked deep in his eyes; she could feel the pain in his heart. Brian had made passionate love to Angel that morning. He was caring, and he gave Angel his heart that day. Brian had showered. Timothy had arrived, and so did Ralph. Ralph and Brian had gone over to Angel's old place and got Angel's furniture. Angel felt good, she was happy; she got up, took a shower, and got dressed. She and Timothy were talking when Brian and Ralph had come back with the couch first. Angel was happy to see that Brian stayed and helped. Brian came in, looked at Angel and told her she looked beautiful; there it was, the Brian Angel was looking for. Brian walked over and kissed Angel. He whispered in her ear and told her he was sorry. Angel smiled and said she was sorry too.

They got all the furniture moved out, and Brian had to leave. He was going to help his daughter Janae' find a car. Brian kissed Angel goodbye. Angel thought, wow, she really needed that. Maybe she and Brian should have more disagreements.

The ring that Brian had gotten Angel was so beautiful. It was oval shaped 2ct. diamond solitaire white gold ring. Angel only liked silver or white gold. It was a pink diamond. Angel was so surprised, but Brian always had good taste in things, maybe not women. Angel laughed at the thought of the other women Brian had entertained. But she just stay focused on becoming Mrs. Ward.

CHAPTER 6:
GOODBYE

Time went on from that day. Angel and Brian said goodbye Angel never thought that goodbye was really going to be the last time she saw Brian. Brian was so good at being distant that Angel started to get used to it, she just stops asking and texting as much. One day Brian came over, and they had a great day. They went to the movies again, and of course Brian fell asleep. Brian and Angel got home from the movies; they got comfortable in the bed. Brian was showing Angel pictures of these house and these barn dominiums. Angel had no clue what those were. Brian asked her if she would live in one. Angel thought they looked really nice, and if that is what he wanted, she was up for it. They talked a lot that night. Finally, Brian put his phone away, and they lay down and made love. The next morning Brian had sat on the edge of the bed, he told Angel that he needed to get things in order, that he may not be able to see that much of her. Angel didn't know where he was going with this, so she just listened. Brian was telling her that he has a lot going on, that he needs time and asked if she could please be patient with him. Angel thought that he just wouldn't be able to come over as much. Hell, she was okay with that; it was going to be hard, but she was trying to be supportive and not act like a spoiled child. She was getting a little used to not seeing him as much. Angel thought at least she would see him one day. Brian told her he didn't know when he could come back to see her. Angel was really confused now. "What do you mean? Brian said, "Baby, please understand. I got to do what I need to do to get my business where I need it to be." Brian told her he wanted to make her happy and give her everything she ever wanted, to not see her work. Angel loved working, but she didn't want to argue with Brian. Angel started to get sad, but she let it go, and she kissed Brian bye. Angel kept feeling uneasy on what Brian told her, so she called him. "Did you mean you can't call me or text me?" He said, "Yes, everything." Angel was hurt because she didn't understand it. Angel tried to take her mind off what Brian told her. She thought he couldn't mean that he loves her. He wouldn't be able to stay away that long. Angel just started cooking. That always made her happy. She made lasagna, she thought back when she first made lasagna. Angel had made Lasagna for the first time.

Brian always comes over now like Angel's apartment is his own he goes straight to the refrigerator. Brian loves hard grapes, so Angel always makes sure she picks some up from the store. Brian grabs some grapes; he sees the lasagna Angel had made on the counter. Angel told him she had never made it before. Brian said that it looks good. They sat down and ate. Brian said, "Baby, this is really good." Angel packed him some to go home with him. Brian was very picky on eating anyone's cooking.

Angel remembers the first time she cooked anything for Brian. Brian had come over; Angel was making chicken, and this was the second time Brian had come over to her house. Angel asked Brian if he wanted some chicken. He said no, but Angel didn't take no for an answer. She grabbed a piece of chicken, sat on Brian's lap, and fed it to him. Angel loves to cook. She was proud of her chicken. Brian said, "Okay, now that's good." That day, Brian had plans for Angel to take her out and show her Atlanta. Angel didn't get out much and didn't really know anything about Atlanta.

Brian and Angel headed out to Brian's car. At this time, Brian was driving an older model Mercedes Benz. That is when Angel noticed Brian was a little untidy. His car had all kinds of junk in it, but she really didn't care. She was just happy to be able to spend time with him. She knew he was a busy man. Angel was excited because Brian had come over early to spend time with her. Angel was going to paint her place, so she needed paint. She had liked the color Brian had painted on his living room walls. Brian was taking her to go buy some paint. They went to Sherman Williams; Brian ordered the color. It was $84 for just one pint of paint. Angel thought that was expensive for paint, but Brian paid for it, and he got the paint supplies as well. Then they went to get something to eat from a restaurant. Brian always sat next to Angel. At first Angel wondered why he didn't sit on the other side, but she liked having Brian near her. Later Brian takes Angel to this club where ladies dance topless. Brian said it was the night the older ladies dance. Angel wondered how he knew this. She figured it was his hang out place. Angel hasn't been to any place like this ever in her life, but she was willing to try for Brian since she was curious about what Brian liked. Angel knew that Brian had a very rare appetite when it came to sex because of the things he was trying to do with her. Angel wanted to be able to please Brian in every way since he was going to be her husband. They pull up to the place. Angel is very nervous, but she goes in. She tries to feel comfortable. Angel notices it was a young lady dancing with no top on. She was a cute lady

Angel thought. Brian was holding Angel in his arms; they both watched the young lady dance. Angel is not sure how she felt. She wasn't jealous or anything. She just felt weird because everyone just acted like it was nothing really, they just carried on. Angel was way out of her comfort zone, but she was willing to try anything for Brian. Brian looked at Angel, kissed her, and said, "You okay?" Angel nodded yes, but Brian didn't believe her. Then off they left. Brian said, "Okay, I can tell you are uncomfortable." Angel had one drink; she was a little tipsy but felt good. Brian and Angel left the club, they were off to wherever Brian wanted to take Angel next. Angel wanted to know why they left the club so soon. Brian said, "I can tell you didn't like it." Angel said she was just trying to take it all in is all. Brian laughed. They drove to downtown Atlanta to the Atlantic Square. Angel was shocked she had heard about this place but never been before. They went to some bar there, got some drinks, and just walked around. Angel thought it was really nice. It was getting really late. Angel couldn't remember the last time she ever stayed out this late. As they were driving, Brian and Angel started talking. Angel wanted to know more about Brian. Brian shared that he used to be a male stripper. Angel thought that was really funny because she felt it. Angel couldn't put her finger on it, but it was like she had seen him before, she knew he did this. It was like Deja vu because she knew she never met him ever, but she told her friend that she felt like Brian was a stripper and she knew him before Brian even told her. Angel never told Brian this she just listens to him tell his story. They talked about a lot of stuff. Angel asked about the twin's mother since the twins were only 1 at this time. Angel wanted to make sure there was nothing still going on. Brian said that the twin's mom and he were co-parenting, and nothing was going on. Brian said that he met her on another dating site and that they were just supposed to be friends with benefits. Angel didn't understand how that would work because she knew that women are emotional beings and eventually, they would develop feelings. Angel listened for a while, and then Brian told her how he was homeless after his divorce from his ex-wife, how he was living in his car and at his business, until he got his house. Brian had plans on moving out of the country, and then the twin's mom called and told him she was pregnant. Brian said he had to talked her into getting an abortion. She had agreed, and they went, but later found out there were twins, so they kept them. Angel picked Brian's brain more because she wanted to make sure she could handle this co-parenting thing. Brian made a mistake about telling Angel that he sits over her house to watch the twins. Angel didn't think that was a good idea now since they were together, so she expressed her concerns. Brian didn't understand why it was a problem, so they sort of got in a disagreement. They go on and on until they pull up to Angel's apartment. Brian and Angel are still having a heated discussion, and they go in. Brian sits down, and Angel is still going. Brian grabs his head, and Angel tells him she just wants to know the truth, so she can make a choice, if this something she wants to invest in. She asked Brian, "What are you doing?" Brian had put his hands on his head and was rubbing his temples. Brian said, "This is my getting pissed off and trying to control myself." Angel wanted to laugh, but she was just trying to get clarification on this co-parenting. Angel just stopped, she went and took a shower. She changed her clothes to something more comfortable. When she came back out, Brian was painting the walls. Angel couldn't believe it. He just painted the entire wall for her; he never said a word. Once Brian was done, he went and took a shower, and they made love and went to bed, like nothing never happened. Brian got up in the morning and took the trash out for Angel. Angel felt bad for even questioning Brian last night.

Angel had wanted those days back so bad, but they were gone, just like Brian gone. She just couldn't believe that. Angel wasn't giving up that easy. She continued to call, text, and video call Brian. Brian would answer most of the time. It was July 4$^{th.}$ Angel was at home just cleaning, trying to stay focused, trying not to think about Brian. Angel's phone rang. It was a number she didn't recognize, but Angel answered it. "Hello ma'am, are you Angel Young?" "Yes, I am." "Ma'am, I am Captain Brown with the United States Air force." Angel's heart was racing because she could tell by his voice something bad had happened to Johnathan. Johnathan was Angel's oldest son; he was overseas in Iraq. "Ms. Young, I am sorry to inform you that Johnathan has been killed in the line of duty." Angel could barely breathe, she went numb. "Ms. Young, are you still there? I am so sorry to have to make this call to you. They will be shipping his body back to the United States tomorrow." Angel was done. She felt lost. She didn't know how she was going to break the news to his brothers and sister. Angel was really feeling lonely. Here it is the 4th, and she lost her son, and she was alone. Angel wanted to call Brian. She thought if she could just hear his voice that it would not be real that her son was gone. "Johnathan is gone!" she screamed and cried, she felt so much pain. She just can't go through this again, first Peter, now her son. "God why? Why me?" Angel cries. Angel is on the bed. She can feel that little girl coming back as she picks up the phone to call Brian; she didn't know if she was going to tell Brian about Johnathan. She just wanted to wait to see what kind of mood Brian was in. "Hello, love, how are you?" Angel said, "I'm good. How are you baby?" "I'm OK. What are you doing?" "I'm leaving momma's house." Brian asked her what she was doing, she said nothing but thinking, Brian said, "Oh, no." Angel knew what he meant by that. Every time Angel thinks, she would question him and pick his brain. Brian hated that. Brian said, "OK let me have it." Angel went on to ask him how come he didn't call her to go with him. Brian said, "I thought you had to work." Angel said, "No, I am off. If you would have called me, you would have known." Brian told her he was sorry, but Angel was getting tired of his sorry. Angel just wanted him to be honest with her. Angel asked Brian, "Don't you miss me?" Brian had this way he would answer things when he lies. He would just say, "Mmmhh," and Angel knew then he didn't. She just wanted to cry. Angel said, "Brian, I just want to spend time with you. Why is that so hard for you to understand? Angel told him he used to spend time with her, that he used to call her and text her all that stuff that happened. Brian told her that is stuff people did in the beginning and things change; people change. Angel couldn't believe those words even fell out his mouth. Angel said, "I didn't change." She wanted to know what changed. "Do you love me?" Angel asked. Brian said yes. She knew that was true, but she couldn't understand why he didn't want to spend time with her anymore, so she kept at him until finally he told her, "You are not the only one I was shitting on." Angel was like, what, what did he freaking say? Brian said that like he was proud he was shitting on her like she deserved it. Angel was so hurt. Brian said that the twin's mom Elizabeth had called his mom, told her how Brian hasn't been helping her out with the twins and other stuff. Angel at first didn't give a care about how Elizabeth felt or how she was getting treated; this was about them. Angel said, "But I thought you told me that watching the twins was one of the reasons why you were so busy because you were spending more time with them." Of course, Brian tried to lie his way out of that one, but Angel wasn't having it this time, so she went on. Then here comes the sad story. Brian said the twins had COVID-19. Angel was so pissed that she totally just ignores it. Brian never tells her anything until he gets in the hot seat. It made Brian mad that Angel just kept going. He got nasty and asked her how could she miss what he is not even doing. Wow, Angel thought, it is true. Brian said he could be an asshole at times and here is Mr. Asshole now. Angel was so upset but also mad, but she calmed herself down and said, "You used to call and do all this stuff. You made all these promises, and every time I hold you accountable, you get mad. I am only asking you for what you said you will give me." Brian said, "How about I just won't promise you anymore?" Angel just got quite now... Angel knew now wasn't the time to tell him about Johnathan; she sure didn't want his pity, nor for him to act like he cared for a day or two then back to the asshole. Angel was done. Her heart was so hurt; Brian was talking to her like he hated her. Angel hated that feeling, she remembers one time Brian had come over to watch the game. He had brought Jeff over with him. Angel was cooking homemade chicken noodle soup. Brian was all nice in the beginning. He kissed her, grabbed her in the kitchen, and started to play with her; he was trying to make her squirt. Brian was always like that with her, he could never keep his hands to himself. Then it was half time. Brian went back to the bedroom. Angel had gone back to the bedroom a little later to just be alone with Brian. It had been a while, as soon as Angel got back there, Brian said, "I knew you were going to bring your nosey ass back here." Angel couldn't believe he said that; she immediately left and went back in the kitchen. Brian came rushing up behind her and pulled her back to the room. Brian had apologized for what he said. Angel didn't know where all this attitude was coming from. She could feel the tension from Brian. The next morning, Brian got up, took a shower, and Angel was still in the bed, lying down, because Brian could always make love making so amazing that it tired her out. Brian all of a sudden had yelled through the bathroom door, asking Angel if she was looking in on him. Angel wondered what the hell was wrong with him. Is he losing his damn mind? Angel's bathroom door didn't shut all the way, and Brian knew that; Angel couldn't figure out where all this accusing her of stupid stuff is coming from. Angel knew something wasn't right. Angel yelled back and said, "No, why would you think that?" Brian just blew it off, but it was bothering Angel. She knew something was wrong. Angel felt it in her gut. It was Brian, he was hiding something, and the guilt was eating him up.

Angel said, "All I wanted was time, the time you said you had." Brian was quiet and told Angel he needed to go because he just had a lot of stuff going on and he didn't want to crash driving on the way home. They hung up with not even saying they love each other. That was the first time Angel felt so empty. She knew that this was really goodbye. Angel had told the kids about Johnathan. She planned the funeral. Angel never told Brian. She just kept it in because she was so lost and hurt, she didn't want Brian's pity or his fake time. Angel had to say goodbye again.

Everyone had left the party. Angel was on cloud 9. She still couldn't believe it. Did Brian really ask her to marry him? She kept looking at her ring and saying, "This can't be." She never gave up, but this was truly her life's dream. She thought back to all those nights she cried herself to sleep because she really felt it was over and he was gone because what he was doing never made sense to her. Angel just looks at Brian and just shakes her head. "You got me,' she said. Brian said, "I know, and don't worry. This is a promise I will keep. You will be Mrs. Ward whenever we set the date."

The days go by Angel is so hurt she just was unable to pull herself together. Angel wanted to give up, but she knew she had to be strong for Mary, Timothy, and Matthew now. Angel just couldn't believe all the mean stuff Brian had said to her. If he only knew her hurt. Angel thought Brian would have called by now so she could tell him what happened. Normally when Brian and Angel would have a disagreement, they would talk; Brian was ignoring her; Angel just couldn't let things go. Angel started second guessing herself and wondering if she should have even called Brian on that night. Angel was so hurt, she was beating herself up with all this regret she felt. She should have shown Brian some compassion for the twins having COVID, but she was hurting too. Brian was so selfish, but she still wondered if she should have just stopped there when he told her, but now she thought, *I had to keep pushing him, and now I pushed him away*. Angel was in tears, just crying every day and night. She didn't know if the tears were for Brian or Johnathan because she was so lost with grief. She needed Brian more than ever now. Angel didn't want to give up; she didn't want to lose Brian too. Angel would continue to call Brian, text him, and video call him. Brian finally answered, he called her Babe, Angel just melted. He told her he was busy, and he would call her back. Brian never called her back. This went on for weeks; it was now around the beginning of August and things still had not gotten any better. Angel was sending letters to Brian. Her emotions were everywhere. She was going through the days just getting by at work, she just tries to stay focused. It helps her to not think about Johnathan or Brian, so she was happy to be at work, but it was the days she was off that killed her. Angel just couldn't let Brian go; she wasn't giving up on them. Brian had sent Angel a picture of him wearing a necklace she had sent him before they had their disagreement. Angel thought he looked very nice. The necklace fit him, but she was sure he wasn't going to wear that one either. Angel wasn't sure why he even sent the picture. She was racking her brain about it. Of course, she texted him and told him he looked nice. Brian would text message Angel back from time to time. Angel felt better that he was calling her baby and queen, so she held onto those words and tried to make herself feel better, but she knew deep down they were just words. The distance and the noncommunication was killing Angel. She would get angry and say fuck him, and then she would cry because she didn't know why he was doing all of this; all she asked for was more time. That is what he said he wanted in the beginning. That was what caught Angel's eye from his profile off the dating site.

Weeks, then months, go by. Angel was losing it. Angel put more into missing Brian than Johnathan. It was easier. She couldn't handle the loss of Johnathan. It just took her soul. Not being able to see his smile and have him come home to spoil her with gifts he would bring back. To hear his stories, he would tell her about the other air force men and women. Johnathan didn't even get a chance to have his own family. Angel hated this. Once again, she had to endure, she just didn't want to think about Johnathan because it was too hard. Angel just kept trying to reach Brian. Brian was coming around a little, he would talk a little more but not much. It wasn't the same. Angel had another plaque made for Brian. She sent it, but she had also sent him this track suit for his logo to see if he liked it. Brian never responded to that package, but he did call Angel back about the plaque. He loved it. They talked a little bit; it gave Angel hope. She was really trying to understand what was really going on with Brian. It is now September; Angel still has not seen Brian. Angel was doing everything to hold it together, but she couldn't because she had a real bad break down. It took all her children to help her get herself back. They would sit up all hours of the night when she was off listening to her cry about Brian. Her children have never seen her this weak, especially over a man. They also knew it was the loss of Johnathan too. Angel hated that her children had to comfort her, she should be comforting them. Even though Angel was hurting over Brian her pain was so great over the lost of Johnathan, she just wanted to not believe it. Angel was hurting bad, her pain for her lost of Johnathan was killing her, it was easy for her to channel that energy into her and Brian, but really, she didn't want to feel anything. It bother her so much because she didn't understand why she couldn't let Brian go, why couldn't she just move on. Her heart was so heavy that she cried for hours and days. Angel made herself sick, she wasn't eating and sleeping. She had lost weight; she just wanted to give up. Angel knew this was not a good example she was setting for her children, especially for Mary, but Angel just couldn't. She just kept thinking about the HIV and who would want her, and how Brian was moving on, and especially losing Johnathan, that really took a toll on her mentally and physically.

Brian tells Angel to not worry about cleaning up because he hired a professional to come tomorrow to clean the house. Brian knew that Angel couldn't sit still in a dirty house because she had OCD bad. Angel smiled. "Okay, now what?" Brian grabs Angel's hand and says, "Come on, Mrs. Ward. Let me give you something to make you fall in love all over again." Brian takes Angel upstairs, and they make love. Angel just can't get enough of Brian. She always thought that it would get boring to Brian, but not to her. Angel enjoyed that Brian still admired her for who she is and still finds her attractive. Angel had struggled so much with being everything Brian needed and wanted in a woman that she forgot her needs. Angel just keeps focusing on her needs now. Losing Johnathan made her realize life is too short. Back then she gave Brian

too much of her energy. Angel wants Brian and her to be one, so giving the same energy back to each other is what has been working so far for Brian and Angel.

It is now in the month of October. Angel still is feeling emotional but a little better. By now her children had enough of Angel's shit, and they were telling her to get over it. They had distanced themselves. Angel felt so bad because she knew her children were grieving to and instead of them being able to grieve, they were taking care of a lovesick crazy woman. Angel thought if only they knew what she was really dealing with, they would understand, but she couldn't bear to tell them about the HIV, especially now after the death of their brother, how Brian had infected her. Angel was still hoping Brian came back. One day Angel was in the shower. She had cried so hard that she couldn't do anything but call on God. Angel immediately started praying harder than she had ever. Angel realized that her connection to God was gone. She put so much into her self-pity and looked for her children to give her what she needed. God was always there for her. Angel prayed and prayed until she started feeling better. As the days went by, Angel could feel herself coming back. Angel had called Brian and told him, "This is stupid. We were together for a year, and we loved one another. Why do you have to be so distant? Why can't we talk like friends? We can at least be friends." Brian said he was just overwhelmed with things; he just needed a break. Angel didn't know what that meant but was still trying to find a way to hold onto Brian. As the days go by, Angel started putting more of her energy back into God, but she still was hoping that Brian would come back. Angel had decided it is time she seek professional help; she found a therapist, at first Angel thought, *this is so stupid. You are allowing a man to send you to get help.* But really, it wasn't just Brian. It was her loss, her hurt over Jonathan. She laughed. "Yep. You are fucked up." All she could do is just honor herself and be honest. She had gotten a female therapist because she feels better with a female than a male. She would go speak with her once every week starting out. Angel started getting her life back, but she still longed for Brian. Angel would go to work, and now she spent an hour in prayer. She would walk, pray, and ask God to either remove Brian from her heart or make him fall to his knees and give himself to you. Angel prayed that every day for God to give her peace. One day Angel was walking, she did her normal prayer. It was almost the end of November. Angel prayed like she normally does, and she heard God tell her that the first will be last and the last will be first. He said that she would elevate above Brian, and Brian would be below her by December, and she would see a shift. Angel didn't know what that meant, but she felt a sense of relief, she could feel her pain start to leave. She called her daughter and told her what was given to her from God. Angel is very close with her children. She shares just about everything, but she just couldn't share with them about the HIV, not yet she thought. Angel gets home, she is feeling really good. She is in a happy place. Peace finally came. She is in the kitchen with her son Matthew talking about today and getting dinner ready. Angel notices she has a message on her phone. It's a number she doesn't recognize. "You don't know me, but I would like to talk to you about Brian Ward. If you could call me back, please." Angel's stomach just dropped, she felt herself get sick. She went to the bathroom and sat there, she immediately started to pray. Angel asked God if this was his plan. "Do I call this person back?" Angel pulled herself together and shut her room door and called the number.

"Hello, my name is Amy. I know you don't know me, and I am not trying to start anything. I was given your name from another lady. I called on this number because I wasn't for sure how this conversation was going to go." Is what the lady said on the other end. Angel was just holding her breath; she didn't want to hear what came out Amy's mouth next. Amy began to tell Angel the story and what took place with her and Brian. Angel wasn't sure she wanted to hear, but Amy was determined to tell it all. Amy asked Angel if she knew if Brian was HIV positive. Angel didn't know what to say. Angel told her she didn't know. Amy told her that he is, and she should get tested. Angel just went along with her; Amy began to tell her story.

CHAPTER 7:

I AM ENOUGH

Angel is still stunned. She just cannot believe she is going to get married. She thought it was a dream until she looked down on her finger and saw that amazing, beautiful ring. Angel was thinking if this really was going to happen. She felt her anxiety start to kick in, she was getting scared. Angel remembered all those promises Brian had made before and how he bailed on her. Angel quickly talked herself out of that negative feeling. She told herself that *Brian is a changed man, and he loves you.* Angel got up, got dressed, and called her mother on the phone. She told her the great news. Angel and her mother talked for hours; her mother was very happy for her. Angel wanted to make sure that her mother would be able to make it to her wedding. She didn't have a date yet, but she told her she would let her know as soon as they set one. Angel had also talked with her two sisters and told them that she wanted them in the wedding. They both were happy and agreed they would. Angel was just so happy but inside a little scared. Angel finally told her

children she wasn't for sure how they would take it, but they all said they just want her to be happy. Things never really worked out easy for her, but she believed this was God's plan all along.

Angel held the phone and began to listen to Amy talk; the entire time Amy was talking; Angel was thinking what God is doing. Amy tells Angel that Brian and she met around June at some conference. They were talking about their goals and dreams for the business they had, and she kind of was feeling him. She told Angel that she had told him that she noticed him on the dating site. Brian told her she should have swiped right. Amy sounded like a very determined, strong woman. Angel just sat back and listened. Amy said that her sister and she were trying to find a new building, they were relocating from Jonesboro, NC and needing a new building. Amy knew where Brian's building was. She said her sister was the one who found the building which happened to be right next door to Brian's building. Angel thought, *Oh, of all the places in Atlanta, you just happen to find a building next to Brian's. Yeah, right.* Amy said that her and Brian had a sexual encounter by this time. Angel was not ready for what Amy had to unleash on her, she took a deep breath in, preparing herself for all that Amy had to say. Amy said that she and Brian fucked a lot and that he put his dick in every hole she had. Angel wanted to pass out. She couldn't believe Amy was telling her this, like she was so proud of it. Amy said that Brian did tell her that he wasn't looking for anything serious, just a friend with benefits. Amy went on and proceeded to tell Angel that Brian would do all kinds of stuff to her he liked anal sex, fucking her in her mouth. Angel was very hurt by all of this because she knew now that Amy was the reason why Brian was distant. He wasn't busy; he was fucking another woman. Angel was getting pissed. She wanted to kill Brian's lying ass. She thought, *Oh, my God. He is a liar.* Amy continues to go into great detail about her and Brian's fucking sessions. Angel wasn't sure what Amy was trying to do, but she let Amy continue on. Amy was sending pictures to Angel from the app that she and Brian were using to communicate. Brian had sent Amy pictures of his dick, and Amy sent pictures of her pussy. Brian told Amy to "come and get all this cum in your mouth and in your ass." Brian was telling her he wanted to fuck her in her ass and put it down her throat. Angel was thinking, *who tells people this shit? What woman tells a stranger how she had sex with a man and sends pictures?* Deep inside, Angel wanted to die, she felt she wasn't enough for Brian, that if she knew more about sex maybe he wouldn't have wanted Amy. Angel continued to listen as she wonders why Amy is calling her now, what led her to call her if she and Brian were doing all this fucking, if they were together. That is because Brian wasn't with her anymore. Amy continued, she told Angel that she had gotten her information from this other woman by the name of Sharon. Amy told Angel that she had found out that Brian was fucking another girl by the name of Kathy. Amy had got upset with Brian because he had come into work one morning with glitter on his face, and Amy said she went off, she told Brian, "What the fuck? Are you fucking that girl? Are you fucking that ugly girl?" Brian told her, "What looks got to do with it?" Amy was so mad that she told Brian, "Nothing since I was fucking your ugly ass." Angel kind of laughed at all of this because this was like some Jerry Springer stuff that you see younger people do, not people in their 40s. Amy was cussing and yelling at Brian, "Does she know you were fucking me? Call the bitch!" Amy wanted Brian to call Kathy on the phone. Brian wanted to know why. Amy told him to "just do it and tell her you were fucking me too." Amy was so mad. "You didn't even have any respect for me, Brian," Amy cried. "You should have respect for your damn self," Brian told her, and that pissed Amy off even more. Angel just listened as Amy continued. She thought, *Oh, my God, this is crazy with a capital K*, but all the time Angel just thought about killing Brian. Brian didn't call Kathy, so Amy got the number and called her. She proceeded to tell her about Brian and her fucking sessions, and she sent her the pictures just like she did with Angel. Kathy didn't care. She told Amy that is between you two. Angel is just sitting on the phone just listening to all this stuff Amy is telling her, she is getting more and more pissed off, but she is more hurt than anything. Amy continues. She hung up with Kathy. She thought she was a simple-minded female. Amy said the next day Kathy and Brian had come to her sisters' job, Kathy had told Brian that Amy kept calling her, Amy denied that she called her. Amy said she wasn't there, that her sister had called her and told her that Brian was up in the shop with some girl. Amy was pissed she said, she got dressed and headed up to her sister's shop. Amy said she immediately went into Brian's gym and started cussing him out. "You brought that bitch to my job? What the fuck?" Amy was going off. Brian told Amy he was going to call the cops; Amy had laughed and said, "Oh that's what you do? Really? You going to call the cops on me? You brought that ugly bitch up to my sister's job. Oh, you got the wrong one. Call the fucking cops. You and her will be the ones going to jail for selling your weed. Fuck you, Brian!" Amy said. Amy was so mad that she stormed out the front door. Amy said she noticed a woman sitting up front, the woman had followed her outside. The woman went up to Amy and said in a timid voice, "Are you fucking Brian? Amy yelled at her and said "Yes, we are fucking." The woman began to cry and said, "I knew it. I knew it, I'm fucking him too. Oh, my God, I knew it." Amy turned to her and said, "Are you Kathy? The woman said, "No, no, I'm Sharon. Oh, my God. I can't let Brian see me talking to you, or he will get me." Amy told her to walk with her to the end of the building. Amy and Sharon began to talk, they had exchanged their numbers. Sharon had told Amy all of Brian's business, how they were together for 4 years, how she was paying his bills. Sharon told Amy that Brian had pictures of a lot of woman on his iPad, that he had sex with a lot of woman. Sharon told Amy that she knows about everything, that her and Brian would have threesomes and do all kinds of sexual activities. Sharon told Amy that Brian was HIV positive, that he was on medicine. Sharon didn't know that she had told the wrong person about Brian having HIV. Amy was really pissed now, and by the time she finished talking with Sharon, Amy had enough stuff to make Brian pay for treating her like shit, and Amy was going to make sure he paid. The next day, Amy waited for Brian. Brian pulled up, got out his truck, Amy yelled, "Brian, you got HIV?" Brian hurried up, unlocked the door, and went into the business; he locked the door behind him to keep Amy out. Amy was so pissed that she started calling all the women that Sharon had given her. That is how she got to Angel. Sharon told Amy that Angel was special to Brian. Amy even called Brian's ex-wife to see if Brian had HIV when they were together, but really, she just wanted to ruin his repetition and tell everyone she could about him having HIV. Brian's ex-wife told Amy that she had to leave Brian because she wanted to live, and be there to see her daughter grow up; she knew all the stuff Brian was in. She told Amy that Brian would have sex with women in the gym, knowing they had cameras up. Angel asked Amy, "So why are you calling me?" Amy tells Angel to let you know to get tested, Angel said, "OK," but inside, she was crying from the hurt because of her secret. Angel couldn't believe all of this; Brian seemed so caring and into positive energy, but he was just full of shit Angel thought. Angel couldn't hold it in anymore, and she just began to cry. Amy proceeded to tell Angel how all this came about. It was around the beginning of November she said her, and Brian had been seeing each other a lot now and having sex in his place of business a lot since she was next door. They would also go to his house at times. She said they had sex around 6 times already. Angel really didn't want to hear any more about them fucking; she was hurt, but she stayed on the phone, she didn't know why, but she did. Amy said that Brian started to get distant; he had stood her up when they had made plans. So, one day around 4:00 a.m., she got a funky feeling in her gut, and she drove up to Brian's job. Amy said she noticed that this female's truck was up there, that she saw coming in the business a lot, but she didn't see Brian's truck. Amy said she went inside, and there was Brian. Amy said she went off, she asked him if he was fucking this other lady and wanted to know whose truck that was. Brian had lied, he told her it was a rental truck. He gave her a sad story. Amy said she fell for the sad story because she wanted to believe him, and she ends up fucking him again she thinks, but she wasn't for sure. Angel thought, *Oh, you couldn't remember then if you fucked him, but you remember all those other times.* Angel was just numb with all of this; she was getting anxious. She just couldn't believe that this was the caring loving father, the man that she fell in love with. She now knew what he held in those sad lonely eyes. Nothing but lies!

Angel calls one of her best friends, Diamond, and she tells her the good news. They immediately start planning her wedding. Angel wants the colors to be emerald green and gold. The theme would be from *The Wiz*, so she wants

the invitations to say ALL OZs on us. Angel and Diamond continue to plan Angel's wedding. They spent up to 4-6 hours on the phone. Angel was so wrapped up in planning. She wanted everything to be perfect, but it wouldn't be perfect because Johnathan wouldn't be there to give her away along with his brothers. Angel just tried to stay positive, as her eyes started to get watery. Angel knew all the key people that would be able to help her. She called Marcy up, so she and Diamond can meet and work together. Marcy was a great planner. Angel was overwhelmed with excitement; she just couldn't believe that God had finally given her, her King. That her and Brian were going to be married. Angel wanted to cry because she remembers the pain, the heartache from the past. She is overwhelmed with joy now.

November 2, it's Brian's birthday. Angel had no clue of all of this stuff going on. She had got Brian a plaque made to remember his dad. Angel had written a poem for him. She wrote it as if it were words coming from his dad; she knew this was going to be hard for him because she knew he had a lot of unanswered questions he didn't get to ask his dad. Angel was hoping it could help him get through this first year without his dad. Angel always thought about Brian. He was more important than anyone at that time.

She had purchased him other things as well. Angel had called Brian that day, she wished him a happy birthday. Angel hadn't talked to Brian for a month, so she wasn't sure how he was going to respond. Brian answers with, "Hello, baby." Angel was so happy to hear him say baby. Angel was still at work; a call had come through from another hospital for her. Angel asked Brian if she could call him back. Brian said, "Yes, baby, I love you." Angel couldn't make out why he was being so understanding and nice. Angel called Brian back. He was still calling her baby, and he told her he loved her again. Angel and Brian talked for about 15 minutes. It had truly been a while since Angel talked to Brian that long. It was good to hear him share how things were going with him. Angel hung up with Brian. She was very happy; Angel had just prayed to God. She had asked God to give her a sign. Brian hasn't called her baby in a while, for him to tell her he loved her instead of her saying it first. Angel was just praising God for answering her prayer. Time went on, and Angel found herself begging Brian to come over to get his gifts. Angel hated that she had to beg a man to come see her or even call her. Angel wasn't no ugly woman. There were men wanting her all the time. Angel had given up on herself because of the HIV; she thought she was nasty. Angel called again. Brian had agreed to finally come over.

November 9, Brian comes over. Angel still had no idea of all that had taken place with Amy, Sharon, and Kathy. Brian looked like he was really tired. His eyes were bloodshot red, and he didn't really look at Angel, but Angel was determined to make this day special. The football game was on the TV. Brian had told Angel to sit down beside him. Angel cuddled up next to Brian, but Angel wasn't used to this Brian. Brian would always touch her and kiss her; he could never keep his hands off her, but now he was barely looking at her. He just rubs her thigh a couple of times. He didn't kiss her; he didn't want to make love or anything; it didn't even seem like he even wanted to be there. Angel overthinks everything, but she continues to be happy, well at least, tries to be. Angel had lost herself. She was so dependent on Brian's validation that she couldn't function unless he approved of her. Angel knew that was so fucked up, she was really a basket case, but she didn't care; she loved Brian, and she was willing to do whatever it took to get him back. Brian finally opened his gifts. Brian really loved the plaque. He said, "It's my dad." He sounded like a little boy, that made Angel cry. She was happy to be able to give him something he could physically hold. Brian sat a little longer, and then he told Angel he had to leave. Angel was hurt, but she didn't let Brian know. She kissed him, but

Brian didn't even respond to her kiss. He just went through the motion. Angel felt like shit. *Why did he even bother to come?* she thought. Angel walked him out the door. Brian had told Angel he had brought a new truck that he wanted to show her. Angel went out to look at Brian's truck. Angel couldn't believe it. Brian had got a drug mobile she thought. He got a black Navigator, he had these huge rims and tires. Angel thought the truck was nice, but it just didn't seem like Brian. It was an attention grabber, like something a young guy in his 20s would get to get those hood girls. Brian showed her he had personalized plates. Angel knew then that Brian was gone. She had lost him to the streets. It hurt her heart, but she smiled and told Brian it was nice and congratulations. Angel's mind was racing as she was walking away. She wanted to cry, she wanted to ask Brian what was going on, why he was treating her like this, what she did to him to hurt him so much that he would be so cold. Angel turns away and walks back up to her apartment. "Angel," Brian yells, "your butt is getting bigger." Angel smiles and says, "It is. Too bad not for you." Brian tells her to shut up.

Angel waits to call Brian; she had to pray and try to take in all the stuff Amy had told her. Angel went to work. Her phone started to ring, there were these numbers popping up. Angel had received a voice mail from an unknown number; it was a woman with a soft voice. The woman was talking about Brian, she was telling her all kinds of stuff some of the same stuff that Amy told her. Angel really couldn't take no more, she had stop listening to the calls . She ran to the bathroom and tried to wash away the tears before they came down. It didn't work; the tears just kept coming. Angel was thinking all this time he never cared or loved her. *How could he?* Brian was a fucking liar; Angel was full of rage. She was hurt and angry. Angel was so pissed because all this time Brian made everything seem to be Angel's fault. Angel was done, but her heart wasn't it still loved. Angel didn't know how to make her heart hate or make it stop loving Brian. Angel beat herself up over this. *How can I still love him he cheated, lied, and gave me fucking HIV? I must be a new kind of stupid female.* Angel thought back to that night he took her to Andretti's again, she just couldn't shake that thought of him giving her HIV on purpose. *Did he give this to me on purpose, so I wouldn't leave him? He knows how I am. Brian was off doing his thing while I am here suffering trying to find myself, trying to get passed this fucking shit growing in me.* Angel cried so hard she couldn't take it. Angel had to take time off work; she was not physically fit nor mentally stable to be able to assist patients. Angel kept thinking, *why wasn't I enough? Why, Brian, why couldn't you just open up and talk to me?* Angel felt the hate growing, she didn't care; she wanted him to pay for all the lies but especially for infecting her with this shit that is growing inside of her. She could barely even say HIV; it made things reality to her when she said it. She still couldn't believe she had it. Angel is in rage of regret. *God, why? Why do you keep putting me through all this pain? Am I even enough for you, father?* Angel is in her bed. The little girl came back again as she picked up the phone to text Brian.

Brian calls Angel. "Good afternoon, Mrs. Ward, how are you doing?" Angel just smiled. She is still overjoyed with the feeling of being loved by Brian. That is all she ever wanted is for him to truly love her. Angel said, "I'm fine, Mr. Ward." Brian said, "I know that Angel smile. What are your plans today, love?" he asked, Angel told Brian that she was already planning the wedding. Brian laughed. "I already knew that". What Brian didn't know is that Angel had already planned this wedding years ago when he first told her he was going to marry her. Angel never got rid of the folder she kept with all the stuff she and Diamond had picked out, so this was going to be done quickly. Brian asked Angel, "Have you picked a date yet?" Angel wanted

it to be on the day that Brian's dad was buried. Angel thought it would be a great way to remember him to always have him there in some way. She wasn't sure if Brian would go for it. Angel told Brian, "No, not yet." She was going to wait for him to come home and discuss it with him.

Angel texted Brian and asked him if he could call her when he got a minute. Brian texted back asking if this was about a Facebook message. Apparently, someone had messaged Brian's oldest daughter Janea' on social media and told her about Brian having HIV. Angel said that it was about a phone call. Brian immediately calls Angel; Angel is in the fetal position, full of tears. Her heart ached; she is numb. Brian said, "Oh, no, baby, what's wrong? Angel told him, "Why, Brian? Why did you lie?" Angel starts to tell him everything Amy said, and what the other lady told her, she said the other lady keeps calling and leaving messages telling her all kinds of stuff. Brian told Angel to change her number, that he would pay for it. Angel said she wasn't changing her number. Hell, they got her number the first time, so what will stop them from getting it again? Angel was just done, she just wanted to die because she was so hurt. She just cried. "Babe, please stop crying. I'm so sorry that they even contacted you. You don't bother no one.

They shouldn't have called you." "But they did," Angel cried. "They did, and it's not about them. It is about you, what you did to even make this happen." By now Angel had talked to Amy so long, she knew everything. Brian wanted to know about the other caller since he already knew about Amy. He asked Angel how the other lady sounded. Angel told Brian that she had a very soft-spoken voice. Brian said that it was Sharon, and he got so mad. He was so hurt that Angel was hurt. Angel cried, "She said you lied, Brian, you lied all this time." Brian said, "I know. I know, baby. Please, I'm so sorry." Angel said, "I am doing everything in my power not to hate you." Brian said, "Please, baby, don't hate me, please." Brian was trying to put the blame on Amy and Sharon by saying they shouldn't have called. Angel yelled "IT'S NOT THEM; IT'S YOU! You shouldn't have fucking lied. You should have kept your dick in your pants!" Angel said, "It's you Brian." Brian said, "I will take the blame 100%, but they didn't have to call you. Baby, you didn't deserve this." Angel said, "you don't know how much I am hurting right now." Brian said, "I can tell. I can hear it in your voice, and I can feel it in my heart. Baby, please don't hate me, please." Angel hung up the phone. Angel cried herself to sleep, and it was hard for her to even sleep through the night. Amy called her again, she began to tell her that Brian took Kathy to the cabins, that she was able to help Brian get money by flipping his $1400 to $14,000. Angel wondered where Brian was getting money from because he started buying her stuff. When she had her car accident, he offered to give her $3000 for a down payment on a car. Angel remembered she was so happy back then, but now she was in a nightmare from hell. She wasn't sure if she wanted to live, she was still trying to survive the nightmare of having HIV and now this. Angel just wanted Amy to stop telling her stuff, but yet Angel hung on the phone, listening to every word, holding back tears. Amy didn't seem to care that Angel was hurting too, that this man promised to marry her, and he gave her HIV. This is the man she trusted with her life. Angel thought, *this is why she is so messed up!* She trusted man, not God! She gave everything to a man, to the world, and the world turned around and fucked her! Angel knew better, but her flesh was weak, she lost herself to this sickness that she held onto Brian. She knew he was lying. She knew he was cheating. All the signs were there. She remembers when she had got pictures of herself made to put on his desk, so one day she came to the gym. Brian told her that he locked the door to his office, that his keys were in his car that got stolen. Brian had told Angel that he was over at the twin's mom's house dropping the twins off early in the morning, that he left the car running with the keys in it. Brian said that he had to feed the twins because their mother was out of town, he was leaving them with their older brothers and sisters. thats when he came back out, his car was gone. Angel didn't really believe him, by now Brian always had a sad story, but Angel didn't like to argue; she just went along with it because she knew eventually the truth would come out. So, the next time she came to Brian's job, time had passed, so Brian had the office door open, Angel noticed her pictures were not there anymore. Angel was pissed, she asked Brian about them. Of course, he had a lie ready, well sort of ready, because he was so good at lying, he could pull those shits out his ass. Brian told Angel at first that he took the pictures home to put in his room, and then he thought about fuck no, she was just over his house. Brian later said, "Oh that's right. They were in the car with all my other stuff that got stolen," and that he was going to take them home. Angel didn't believe him, so then Brian flipped it, told Angel to stop it, don't do this, that he has enough to deal with that he couldn't take this negative energy right now, so Angel sucked it up and let it go, but she knew he was full of shit. Once again, she lost herself to not being enough. Angel gave up on being loved, and settled for what Brian gave her, just enough to keep her hanging on.

Angel listens as Amy tells her that Brian also spent his birthday at a restaurant with Kathy. Angel just cried; she didn't care anymore about what Amy thought. She cried and screamed, "Oh, my God! Why!". Brian could never do anything with her anymore. "I gave that man everything. I supported him. I motivated him!" Angel just kept going over and over in her head how many times she begged Brian to go to the cabins and how she would plan trips for them, how he would always have an excuse why he couldn't go. Angel thought, *why wasn't I good enough for the cabins?* Angel was thinking all of this as Amy was saying she was better than Kathy and Sharon, that Brian could have had everything with her. Amy said she was the best thing he could have been with. Angel knew she also thought she was better than her too. Angel didn't care; she felt the same way. Because Brian left her to go be with Amy. Angel lost herself to not being enough. Amy went back to her fucking sessions with Brian. that is all she had, but Amy didn't want to believe it; she wanted it to be more than just a fuck, she didn't want to look like a thot, so she bragged about how when she sent the pictures of Brian's dick to the other women, that Brian sent the picture of her pussy to her, she told Brian, "My pussy looks good; it can be put in a magazine. You know you love my pussy." Amy said she thought she was better than the other two because she knew she had a good fuck game; Angel knew she was also included too as well. Amy tried to ask Angel about her and Brian's sex. Angel told her, "We made love. We hardly ever really fucked. He always made passionate love to me." Angel said, "I guess he just wanted to fuck someone. I don't know." Angel wondered why Amy sent pictures of Brian's dick to these other women. Clearly, they already knew how his dick looked since he had fucked them. Angel knew it wasn't the picture of Brian's dick that Amy wanted them to see. It was what he said that made her feel special. He was telling her to come get this dick and how he wanted her pussy and all that stuff. It made her think she was special. Angel was done; she was empty. Each word Amy said took life from her. But what really got Angel was what came out of Amy's mouth next, she said she thinks Brian is the devil because he took her soul, and that is why she couldn't get him out of her system. She told Angel that Brian had done this breathing thing. Angel just dropped the phone, she wanted to die. She thought that was something special her and Brian had. Nothing was special; it was all lies. Angel was numb. Amy said she had spent the night over Brian's house, one night her phone went off. Amy was a Muslim, and her phone played her chant when it went off. She said that

Brian waited till the next day and went off on her about how she brought that shit in his house, that he didn't like that energy. Angel was still thinking about the breathing. she was done, she couldn't take no more. Angel told Amy she had to go; she had heard enough; she just couldn't take no more. Amy still wanted to share, so she kept talking about how Brian fucked her in his gym, how he fucked her while she was on her period. Angel was just getting sick, she said, "I really need to go, Amy. It's late, and I need to sleep." Amy said, Are you okay? Are you okay?" Angel wanted tell her, *What the fuck you think? You just told me the man I thought I was going to spend the rest of my life with has fucked you well and how much he enjoyed your pussy over mine.* Angel just told her, "No, but I will be. I just need to pray."

Angel got off the phone and called Brian. She sounded like that little girl now. She was so hurt that she asked him, "You took Kathy to the cabins?" Brian said yes that his brother had introduced Kathy to him, that it wasn't nothing, that he came up there with his brother and sister-in-law. Angel knew he was lying. To think just because she didn't like to argue, he really thought she was stupid. She told Brian to stop lying, that she couldn't take it, she wondered how he could do that. "Brian, you promised me that you were going to plan a special trip for us because you missed my birthday. You fucking promised me. Angel was so hurt after all she had done and how much she had been there for him. She gave her heart, and he just shitted on her. Angel asked him about the birthday dinner. She really didn't want to ask, but she did. Once again, Brian lied. He told her that his brother was surprising him, that they invited Kathy, that she was just a friend. Angel just cried because she was thinking that he was out there having fun, no concern about the poison he left her with. She wanted to kill him; she felt that hate building up. Brian never called to check on her to see if she was okay or even went with her to one of her fucking appointments. Brian was just a selfish asshole, Angel wanted to hate him; she wanted to forget she ever met him. She thought about how this happened, about how she could have been so stupid, her of all people. Angel hung up the phone since she could tell Brian could give a fuck. She cried and cried; this went on for days. Her son Matthew tried to comfort her, but he was full of rage himself. He wanted to kill Brian for hurting his mom. Matthew really thought Brian was a good guy at first until he stopped coming around, but he wanted to believe because he wanted his mother to be happy. Matthew was trying everything he thought of that night, he allowed his mother to lay in his arms. He became her shoulder to cry on, he held her all through the night because he knew his mother was empty; she had given up the fight. Matthew was always used to seeing his mother strong. He never saw his mother like this, and it killed him that he couldn't fix it. He couldn't make her feel better because she was always making everyone else feel better, even that bastard Brian he thought. Matthew held Angel tighter as he fought back his tears. Just then he heard his mother say, "Brian gave me HIV." Matthew couldn't let go of her. He rocked her as he cried even more as thoughts of how he was going to kill this mother fucker ran across his head. Matthew loved his mother with everything in him, this took his breath away. He couldn't share his thoughts with Angel, so he just sat quietly holding her tight, but he thought if anything happened to his mother Brian would pay. Matthew didn't care; he was going to fuck his life up. Angel faded away in Matthew's arms; all she could do is dream that it was Brian who was holding her. She still longed for him; she questioned herself, she had beat herself up to why. Matthew told her, "It's OK, Mommy. Stop beating yourself up. The heart wants what the heart wants. We have no control over who we love. We love and hope it all works out." Angel looked at Matthew, she wondered how the hell he got so smart. She thought it was the weed he was smoking, but it made Angel feel a little better. She stopped thinking about being good enough. Matthew said, "Brian was the one who wasn't good enough for you because he let go of a rare breed. You are a diamond. You are gold. He is missing out, not you. Angel felt very special to hear Matthew describe her like that. Angel found a little peace, and she fell asleep in Matthews' arms.

Brian had reached out to Angel to check on her to see if she was okay. Angel was still in pain, so she didn't answer his call. Angel texted him, she told him she was hurt so bad. "How could you do this to me? What happened to all that loyalty? You kept talking about all this shit about positive energy." Angel said, "You took the last of me. I have nothing left to give." Brian said he wanted to just die. Angel wanted to tell him she would give him the fucking bullets to kill himself, but she knew she was just hurt. One thing Angel vowed was she would never speak out of anger; you never can take back your words especially if they're hurtful. Angel told Brian she wants to die too. Angel never felt heartache like this, she figures it must be true. Brian must be her first true love because she just couldn't find the strength to go on. Brian kept apologizing and telling Angel that Sharon and Amy were just jealous because she was special to him. He told her everyone knows how special she is. Angel didn't really care what everyone thought. It was what Brian thought, what he showed her, and he showed her that she was nothing, that she wasn't ENOUGH!

CHAPTER 8:

ONLY GOD

Brian had come home. Angel had dinner waiting for him. Brian prayed over the food, and they began to eat. Angel asked him how his day was because Brian seemed a little uneasy. Brian began to tell her that something bad had happened at one of the locations. One of the trainers was having sex with a client at the job, and she reported him said he had raped her. "Oh, my God!" Angel said, "Who?" It was one of the older trainers, Brett. Brett had been with Brian since he had started his second location. Brian was hurt, he couldn't believe it; Angel couldn't either. Angel asked what was Brett saying. Brian said that Brett was denying the allegations, but still, it was not a good look for the business at all. Angel was trying not to think back to when the shit hit the fan with Amy. It was terrible for Brian, and Angel knew Brian was thinking the same thing. Angel told him, "Don't worry, baby. If it is not true, God will work it out. I will pray for the truth to be revealed." Brian said,

"No, we will both pray." Angel smiled and said, "Yes, we both will. I believe it will all be okay. Your business will not be affected by this." Angel walked over and held Brian, she placed his head in between her breasts. "It's okay. God's got us; you know this." Brian said, "How the hell did I get so lucky? You always did lift me up. You gave me so much peace, and support, you will never know how much you mean to me. I could never know how you even knew sometimes when I was hurting." Angel said, "God told me, remember, you said we were connected." It's funny. Angel felt the same way about Brian. He would call or text her at the right time like he knew. Even when he was around her, he would know if she was hurting. The connection was strong, and God tied them together. Brian went upstairs and took a shower; Angel had cleaned the kitchen. She thought that this was not the time to bring up the wedding date. Angel went upstairs. Brian, to her surprise, was so ready for her, Brian had stood up, buck ass naked, his dick just nice and hard. He was ready. Brian looked Angel in her eyes. "Do you love me?" Angel almost came right there, she smiled. "Yes, forever and ever. I will love you to death do we part." Brian was taking Angels clothes off. He had slowly run his hands across her breast. By this time Angel's nipples were so hard she could feel herself getting wet.

Brian had pulled down her sweatpants. As soon as he touched her between her legs, Angel let out a moan. She could feel the wetness trickle down. Brian smiled and said, "That's my girl." Brian kissed Angel so gently, yet very passionately. He whispers in her ear, "You're not going nowhere; we will be together forever." Angel felt the tears start to flow. She can feel her heart racing. Brian picks her up, lays her on the bed. Brian just stares at Angel, he tells her, "You are so beautiful. How could I have treated you so bad? You're my Angel." Brian then lays his hard body on her as he slowly goes down and kisses her body. He teases Angel as he kisses in between her thighs. Angel is getting so aroused she can't wait for Brian to enter her. Angel feels herself cum, the juices start to flow. Brian knows Angel's body very well; he always did. He starts to lick her, Angel just explodes. She could no longer hold back, she cries, "Brian please, please." Brian continues to lick. He does it so slow that it drives Angel crazy. Her legs start to shake; she can feel herself starting to fade away. "Brian, I can't" she says. Brian says, "You can't what?" as he continues to lick her pussy so slow and making sure he hits it just in that right spot. He can feel her clit get harder and harder. Angel is going crazy. "I can't take it, Brian! Brian!" she cries out. Brian says, "Yes, baby!" Angel is speaking in her heavenly language again. Brian tries so hard to figure out what she is saying, but he just enjoys the pleasure he is giving her. Brian kisses Angel on her lips as he pushes his hard dick inside of her. Angel cries out, "Brian, it's going to happen. It's about to happen!" Brian knew what that meant. Brian continues to push even deeper and deeper. He can feel all of Angel's juices flow down his dick. Brian is enjoying this feeling; he is enjoying making love. His emotions are all into pleasing Angel; he was never so in tune to the feeling of making love before because with the others, he would just be doing the act. It was a want to him not a need, but he needed Angel to feel complete; he needed to feel her love because he needed her. Brian knew that she was real. She didn't just want his big dick. She wanted all of him, the good the bad. She stood with him, accepted him, the broken him. Brian thought about how Angel was so given to his children and to him, Brian started to get emotional as he pushed deeper and deeper. Angel could hear Brian's heartbeat faster and faster. Brian was pushing and pushing, Angel was crying out, "Yes, Brian! Yes, baby I'm all yours!" Brian said, "Give me that wet pussy. Cum for me, baby!" Brian cried out. Angel was breathing heavy now. Brian was pushing his hard dick in deeper and deeper; he was starting to pick up the rhythm. He was going faster and faster. Angel is crying, "Oh, my God! I'm cumming! I'm cumming!" Brian feels himself starting to release his entire soul in Angel. Brian suddenly places his mouth on Angel's and tells her to breathe. Angel takes a deep breath in. It takes her soul. She enters Brian, and Brian enters her; together they became one. Brian gave one final push as he unleashed all his cum inside of Angel. Angel squirted everywhere; Angel knew then that God had truly placed them together. Brian and Angel laid in peace and went off to sleep.

Days went by. Angel was just walking in a daze. She just was hoping all of this was a dream, that she would wake up and she and Brian would be back laughing and joking. But it wasn't a dream. It was a nightmare; she was scared of what would become of her and Brian. Amy had called Angel to tell her that she was scared. Amy was so worried about catching HIV from Brian. Angel knew Brian was on his medication. Well, she wasn't 100% sure. But she didn't think Brian wanted to die, she told Amy that she had nothing to worry about since she had already been tested. Amy had already had a test done, and she was negative. Angel was getting pissed that Amy would always go back to her past about her ex having HIV, how scared she had been.

Angel thought that she wasn't that damn scared that she didn't use a condom when her and Brian had sex. Amy told Angel that she had brought condoms over to Brian's house, but she didn't use them. Angel said, "You are fine, just relax." Once again Amy felt the need to keep bringing up how Brian and her would have sex, and each time the story would change. Angel felt that Amy was competing with her, trying to see if Brian cared more for her or Angel. Amy knew that Brian just was using her for sex and for whatever else he could get out of her. Amy told Angel, "Oh did you know that Brian and Kathy are flying out of town?" Angel knew it, that is the real reason why Amy was calling to make sure that Angel felt the same pain and hate like she did. Angel took a deep breath and said, "No, I didn't know and don't really care." Angel cared but wasn't going to let Amy know she did, Angel was just numb. Angel got off the phone and just prayed. Then another call came in from an unknown number. Once again, the timid voice lady spoke. Angel was done, she wanted to be left alone. Angel video called Brian. He answered. He was in a store, and it looked like he was shopping. Angel was in tears. He said, "Baby what is wrong? Angel told him they keep calling. He said, "Baby, just ignore them." Brian told her, "They are just jealous because they know you are very special to me." Angel didn't feel it. "How could I be special when you didn't give a fuck about me, just out fucking everyone." Angel could never really express her feelings to Brian; she just held it all in. Angel was done. Brian said, "Baby, I will get to the bottom of it. I will get them to stop. Please, baby just don't hate me." Brian tried to call Sharon on the phone, but she didn't answer, he was pissed. He wanted her of all people to leave Angel alone. Brian knew he couldn't control Amy. Amy was a force to deal with, she was determined to make him pay. Angel hangs up with Brian, she tries to just get by. Angel had not prayed for some time now. Angel realized that she had lost God. She was so busy trying to find comfort in people, her children, friends when all she needed was God. Angel began meditating and getting back in tune with herself, her connection with God. Angel started reading the Bible more, she would focus on positive energy. She was in the middle of praying when Brian called her to check on her; it sounds like he was in an airport. Angel asked, "Brian are you going out of town with Kathy?" With no hesitation Brian said yes. Angel didn't think she had any more tears, but they started to flow. "Brian, why?" she asked. Brian said he was going to help her drive a car back. Angel remembers what Amy said about him flying out, she wonders how the hell Amy knew they were flying out. Angel said, "Are you and Kathy together?" Just then she heard the little lying voice come out his mouth. "Mmmhh." Angel knew that Kathy must have been sitting next to him. Angel just hung up the phone and cried. She had nothing, so she prayed God give me peace.

That night Angel's phone was blowing up. Amy and Sharon were calling, now that Angel figured out who the unknown number belonged to. Angel didn't want to talk to anyone but Brian. Angel was texting Brian, but he didn't reply. Angel was getting pissed. Brian always answered her calls. Brian never called or texted Angel back. Amy was still calling. Angel had finally answered the phone. Amy was pissed and needed to unleash her emotions. She couldn't believe that Brian was with Kathy. Amy thought she was so ugly. Amy was just going off, saying she could have given Brian more. She could do all this stuff she was bragging how she is the better one again. Angel really didn't want to keep hearing this. Amy started talking about how she still needs to get tested. Angel wanted to say, "Stop! You don't have it. I do!" Amy told her she was concerned about the other women he is having sex with. Amy told Angel she was calling these women, asking them if they knew Brian had HIV, if they were sexually active with him. Amy just wanted to tell them all about Brian's HIV status, trying to ruin his reputation to get back at him. Angel just sat and listened, she asked Amy why she felt she needed to do that. Angel was pissed at Brian as well and felt he needed to pay but she knew God will have the last say not her. She was hurt that he wasn't responding to her text messages, she felt that evil spirit that Amy had taken root in her. She was on board to Brian paying for his actions, so she continued to listen. Amy said she had called this one lady; she was a pole dancer. Angel held her breath because she knew who that one was. Amy said she called her, she asked her about her and Brian's relationship, she asked her if she knew that Brian was HIV positive. The lady told her no and that she appreciated that Amy was standing up for all the women Brian had slept with. Amy said the pole dancer lady told her that she should report him if she feels he is doing this. She told Amy that she didn't benefit anything from Brian. Angel felt her heart sink, she knew Brian had been sleeping with her as well. Angel wondered if she had HIV too. Angel was getting overwhelmed; with all these women Brian had been sexually active with she was getting sick to her stomach. Amy was just going on and on. Angel said, "Okay, Amy, I have to go. I need to sleep," but really, she wanted to just ball up in the bed and cry herself to sleep. Angel knew it didn't matter how much she hated Brian. Her heart still wanted him. Angel wanted to rip her heart out, so she just started to meditate and pray.

Father, hear my cry; I want to die. I can't take this pain.
My heart is so heavy with grief, can you please give me peace?
I struggle with all of this mess, that hate consumes me. I want him to
Pay for how he used me. He took from me, left me with this sickness,
That the bitterness eats away at me. I'm losing myself to self-pity.
I don't even know me. Anger and rage are my true friends; they comfort the
Hate that grows within. Please, father, can you give me peace help me to
Understand why this man, why me? I can't eat or even sleep. Visions
Of him and me play in my head to only awake to nightmares of all
The women he had. Please, father, I grow weak. You said if we call on you

You will give us everlasting peace, so here I am, father,
your child crying out.
Please hear me.

That night, Angel prayed with everything in her. She wanted God to free her from all this pain, she cried and cried till she finally went to sleep. It was early in the morning when Angel's phone went off. It was Brian returning her text message. Brian then called her said he had arrived home to a lot of shit. Angel didn't know what was going on, she really didn't care since he didn't care that she was at home hurting while he was out enjoying himself with Kathy. He didn't even give her a thought. Angel was so pissed that she couldn't give Brian that same positive energy that he loved about her. Angel became bitter, she was trying to not hate, but it was feeling so good to hate him, to see him pay. Angel listened to Brian as he told her that Amy had put a notice on his door saying that it's against the law for him to not disclose his status of HIV. Angel wanted to laugh right in Brian's face and tell him that's what he gets. Angel wanted to be that bitch for once. Angel listens as he tells her there is so much shit going on right now. Angel didn't care. Why should she? He didn't care about her feelings or anyone for that matter. Angel told

Brian, "Well, she was the one you left me for." Brian told Angel he didn't leave her for Amy. "Then what do you call it Brian? You said you didn't have time, but in fact, you did have time, just not for me. So, you gave crazy my time." Karma, Angel was just done. Brian had lied so much to Angel that she was becoming so angry, she could feel the emotions overtake her. She was feeding that hate; she knew she had to hang up before she said something very bad.

Angel got off the phone, she felt a little relief knowing that Brian was feeling hurt like she was. Amy called Angel, she was telling her how she and Sharon had gotten into it. Amy said that Sharon had called her, she told her, "Why can't you just let it go; you're not infected, so move the fuck on." That pissed Amy off. Amy said she knew Brian put her up to it if he wasn't on the other line listening. Amy had gone to the police department, to see what her options were because she wanted Brian to pay, she felt she was helping all the other females. That is why she called Angel; Angel gave Amy some type of peace in a weird way, she told Angel that she was going to press charges against Brian. Angel was just tired of the entire thing. Angel asked Amy about the notice she put on Brian's house door. Amy laughed and said, "Oh, he's back. I wonder if Kathy saw it, wonder what she thought." Amy hated Brian, but Angel knew better. She knew that Amy really wanted Brian to be with her. Angel can feel evil spill in her veins, she didn't like this feeling. She told Amy, "I'm going to go now." Angel started to pray again; Angel found herself praying every day now. Angel didn't want that hate in her, she wanted to be free and have peace, so she meditated. Angel would wake up each morning with worship and given thanks to God for peace. Angel could feel that bitterness fall from her, she was even walking differently. Angel had returned to work; she was going through her day. She took her lunch breaks; she would just walk and pray just thank God. Angel realized that she had to go through all of this because she had put Brian before God. She felt God was trying to get her attention, that is why he took Brian away. Angel was sad, but her heart was healing, she was finding peace. This became Angel's routine: waking up, praying, meditating, and just asking God to use her to be a blessing to someone. Angel didn't want Brian to go to jail, she didn't want his children to be embarrassed by what their father has done. Angel knew she had to continue to help by allowing Amy to find the peace she needed through her. Maybe she would just let it go, so once again she stood in to help Brian. Angel started to pray for Brian. She asked God to remove all that negative energy out of him and fill him with peace to restore him and make him a changed man. She asked God again if Brian is not the man for her to remove him from her heart, but if he is the man for her, then allow him to fall on his knee and confess you lord as his savior. Brian didn't believe in God, so Angel was pretty much ready for God to take Brian out her life. Angel had just got this sense of peace fall on her.

Brian rolled over. He kissed Angel on her forehead, told her he loved her, and then went to take his shower. Angel just rolled over, smiled, and took a sneak peek at Brian's sexy ass. *Thank God, you blessed me with this sexy man,* **she thought. Brian left for work. Angel had got up to get her day started. Angel had planned a lunch date with Diamond and Marcy to do the final preparation for the wedding. Brian was at work, trying to put out the fire that Brett had caused. Brian was really hurt by this because he knew what he had gone through with his stupidity back in the past. It almost cost him everything, especially Angel. Brian had set up a meeting with Brett, so when Brian had arrived in the office, Brett was sitting there waiting. Brian was so hurt because he had to let Brett go because it was just too much of a risk since he broke policy. Brian made sure that all his trainers signed an agreement, male or**

female, that said you could not have any sexual relationship with any of the clients. Brian listened to Brett as he had explained what took place with Trina, the lady who accused him of sexual assault. Brett said that Trina and him had started seeing each other about two weeks ago. Brett said it really wasn't nothing but sex to him. Brian shook his head because he knew from what happened with him and Amy, it is never just sex. Brett said he was trying to end it and move on with someone else. Trina got pissed. Brett said he never raped Trina. Brian said, "ok, well you had signed the policy stating that you would not have any kind of sexual relationship with any client, so I have to let you go. You really leave me no choice. You put me in a bad situation Brett, and this hurts me." "I know, man, and I apologize. I totally understand. I blame myself for being so stupid, thinking with my dick; it will get you all the time."

Angel was feeling so much better. She would put God first; She and Brian had been talking more. But Brian was still out there. Amy told Angel that Brian was selling marijuana. Angel wondered how she knew all of this stuff. Angel was just trying to stay focused on what God is trying to do. She was getting rid of hate and finding that peace. Angel was still wanting Brian; she couldn't let go of what they shared in the beginning, and she couldn't believe that it was all fake that Brian didn't care. Angel just kept praying and believing that God will reveal the truth. One day Angel was just so weak that she just wanted to be in Brian's life, it didn't matter how. Angel texted Brian, she told him that she would like it if she could be in with him, Kathy, and Sharon. She wanted to be in the triangle. Angel was so nervous because she knew that Brian was into a lot of sexual stuff, she had no clue about. Angel just wanted to see Brian to be in his arms. She didn't care if she had to share him. She had read about stuff like this, she thought she could do it. Brian had told Angel, "You in the picture would be great." Angel smiled, and she felt good for a couple of days. Brian had given Angel money to get her feet done. Brian wanted her to send pictures because he knew how she got when it came to her feet. Brian would always take care of her; all she had to do was ask him. Brian never told her no; he gave her whatever she wanted. Angel really didn't ask him for much because all she wanted was his time. That is something he couldn't give her. Angel was still praying and asking God for peace, she knew that this was wrong, but she just wanted to have Brian. Once again Brian became her main concern. Angel just cried, "Please take this out of me. I can't. I can't, father. This is too much." Angel sent a long text to Brian that night God told her she could not entertain what Brian is doing. Brian read the text. 'That is deep. I need help. I'm so broken right now. I am lost. I am torn, and I'm full of regret to the point that I am sick. You are everything to me and more you are a true angel, and a blessing to everyone you love. I need to get the help I need." Brian texted that back to Angel. Angel just cried and thanked God; she knew God was working.

It's December now, and things with Brian and Angel are going pretty good. Brian had texted her and said, "Good morning, Queen." Angel felt good to hear that but really wanted to have Brian lying next to her. Angel was getting so lonely. It was cold, she was feeling a little horny. She longed to feel Brian's hands on her body. She was laying in the bed, imagining him touching her and kissing her before Angel realized she was getting aroused. Angel began to take her hands and rub them down her breast and imagine it was Brian's hands touching her. Angel took her fingers; she began to touch herself. She could feel Brian reaching in between her legs. Angel is getting wet; she could feel her heart racing as she continues to stroke her wet pussy with her fingers. Angel calls Brian's name as she can feel herself about to cum. She is in tears now she is so ashamed because of wanting Brian so much; she began to pray to ask God to forgive her. She hates how much she loves this man. Angel hated that she felt this way when Brian was out with someone else clearly, he was moving on. Angel cried, she took a deep breath in and got up she started her praise and worship. Angel was at work when she received a call from Amy. Amy told Angel that she had spoken with the police again, and she was thinking about filing a complaint against Brian. Angel thought, *here we go again*. Angel didn't know what to feel or say, so she just listened. Amy told her that she couldn't take it no more, that God put her here to use her and it is her job to do this. Brian needs to pay for what he did, now Amy is saying he violated her. Angel just shook her head; Amy was going off and crying, saying it just isn't fair that he can just go around being happy while other people are worried about their health. Amy said she is going to put in a report tomorrow that Brian needs to pay. He is a liar, a manipulator, and he is selfish, he doesn't care about anybody but himself. Angel didn't say a word because she believed what Amy was saying was true. That night Brian texted Angel he was telling her he was having a hard time, and he just needed to sleep. Brian asked Angel if he could come over. He didn't want to sleep at his place. Angel was so happy, she believed God was answering her prayers. She told Brian yes, she sent Brian her new address because she had moved since all of this stuff had happened, she wanted a clean start. Angel asked Brian if he wanted anything to eat Brian told her he didn't have an appetite. Angel told him she would just make something anyway just in case he did. Brian said he needed a hot shower and just sleep. Angel said okay, as much as she longed to have Brian make love to her, she would rather have him just hold her and whisper in her ear to tell her he still loved her.

Brian arrives and knocks at the door. Angel had just finished praying, she was so nervous. It was like the first day she met Brian. Her heart was racing, she couldn't wait to see him. Angel opens the door, and she sees this weak little man. Brian had lost a lot of weight; he did not look like the strong Brian she was used to seeing. He looked so helpless; he looked a hot mess. Angel couldn't believe how bad he looked. Brian walks in. Angel showed him where the shower was. Angel goes off and starts to cook. She made him some shrimp pasta noodles with alfredo sauce. Angel comes into the room. Brian is knocked out. She looks at him for a minute. She just wanted to kiss him, hold him in her arms. Brian looked so peaceful, so innocent she didn't want to wake him. Angel thought about waking him by kissing him, but she remembers that last time she kissed him he barely even kissed her back. Angel leans over Brian and whispers in his ear, "Brian, Brian here is your food." Brian wakes up, he asked her what she made. Angel told him, he said, "baby, you gave me too many noodles." Angel thought that was so cute how he said that. Brian ate his food and off the sleep he went. Angel climbed in the bed she didn't know if she should be naked or what, so she just had her panties and tank top with no bra. Brian had rolled over and grabbed Angel. He held her tight. Angel was at peace; she was able to get the best sleep ever. Brian woke up early. He grabbed Angel and began to rub her breast. Angel could feel her nipples get hard, she started to breathe hard. Brian said, "What's wrong baby? Angel said, "You know." Brian said, "yes, I do," and did a little smirk and off he went to get dressed. Brian took Angel in his arms. He held her tight and told her he loved her, and then he left. Angel returned to bed. She was tired, she didn't understand why she was so tired. It was like Brian had taken all her energy away. It felt like they had sex. Angel thought that was weird, she thought maybe their spirits had sex. Angel slept until 3 p.m. Brian texted her, he thanked her for letting him stay. He told Angel he was in a better place now. Angel was so happy she could give him peace.

It was Christmas, and Angel wondered if Brian was with Kathy. It would hurt her if he were because he was just over at her house. She was waiting for Amy since Amy always knew everything. Angel felt it in her spirit that he was. She started feeling sick. She didn't understand why he even came over to lay with her if he had her. Angel was so confused, so she prayed and hoped it wasn't so. Angel and Matthew were out grocery shopping when Angel got the call she dreaded from Amy. Amy sent a picture of Kathy looking like she was riding in Brian's truck, saying Merry Christmas. Angel wanted to break down right there, but she just kept going. She didn't want Matthew to know she was hurting; she didn't want him to be filled with anymore hate. They get home. Angel puts the groceries away, she is singing, praying, asking God to give her strength. Amy sent another picture. It was a little video of Kathy talking about something. Angel just didn't understand why Amy would go through all this trouble to find this stuff, but she knew Amy was hurting too, but most of all, Angel just thought she was crazy. Angel couldn't understand why Brian keeps doing this to her. *Doesn't he know that he is causing me to want to hate him?* Angel just prays because she refuses to give into this negative energy she is feeling, so she doesn't even reply to Amy's text. Amy texted Angel and told her, "See, I told you that mother fucker doesn't care about anybody but himself. He doesn't care about you either, Angel." Angel was hurt, but she was right; he couldn't care, but she couldn't get past the night he came over and held her. Angel continued to pray, she asked God for confirmation. She needed to know if Brian is the one, and she needed to know the truth. *God, give me peace* is all Angel could ask. That is what she prayed every day. *Peace fall fresh on me*. Brian hadn't even text Angel to say Merry Christmas. Angel was trying to stay strong, but she felt her heart melting away. Angel continued to just push through the day. Angel had started working out with her brother Ralph, they started having a daily routine. Ralph had lost his job; this is the 3rd time he has been out of work. Ralph has been off work now for almost a year. Ralph got in a car accident on the job, so he was on worker's comp. The company that he was working for at the time had let him go, so Ralph had nothing but time. Ralph was an excellent trainer, but he just liked to talk a lot, and he lied a lot. Angel laughed because she thought he and Brian had that in common too. Angel was feeling much better about herself, she was getting Angel back, but she still missed Brian, she would wish Brian were with her, so they could work out together. Angel remembers when Brian had come over, and they went to the gym together to work out. It was so much fun she thought. Brian couldn't keep his hands off her, but they managed to get some training done. Now she couldn't get him to put his hands on her. Ralph would record some of the workouts. Angel would post them on her social media, a lot of people enjoyed the videos. They would tell Angel that it motivates them to want to go work out. Angel liked the feedback; it kept her working harder on getting her body right. It also kept her busy, so by the time she came home, she was tired, she really didn't have time to miss Brian. One day Angel was doing her normal Friday training she had to do on zoom. She was just finishing up the training when she got a text from Brian. He had asked her how she was doing. Angel was not in a good mood; she was just trying to understand why things had to go the way they did. Angel would get mad at herself and blame herself for the way things were going. Angel replied by saying, "I'm in a bad place right now." "That is not what I wanted to hear," said Brian. Angel was just thinking that maybe she was just too nice, maybe she should have cursed Brian out instead of trying to be a peacemaker. Brian told Angel that she is like the sun. "When you are down or sad, it's like the sun goes behind the clouds." Brian told Angel that when she hurt, he could feel it in his stomach; it makes him sick. Angel was moved by what Brian had said, it made her feel a little better. Angel was just happy Brian had reached out to her.

Brian didn't want Angel to have any more contact with Amy. He told her that Amy was negative energy, he didn't want Angel to have no part of that energy. Angel told Brian that she had to stay in contact with Amy, so she wouldn't press charges against Brian. Angel didn't want Brian to lose what he built, nor did she want his family to have to go through the embarrassment of knowing that their father was doing all of this. Angel just listened to Amy rant on about pressing charges and how Brian should have been with her. Angel had started to find peace with things. Amy had been trying to set up a meeting with Angel, so they could talk in person. Angel didn't know why the hell they really needed to talk in person, but she was willing to do anything that would make Amy stop. Brian really hated that he had put Angel in this situation; it was killing him. Angel had agreed to meet with Amy on Saturday, so Angel drives out where Brian works because Amy's shop is right next door. Angel wanted to see Brian too; she had made him some food. Brian had texted Angel to see where she was as Angel had just pulled up to the building. Brian wasn't there. Angel tried texting, but her text wasn't going through for some reason. Angel decided to go over to Amy's place of business. Out comes this fairly tall looking, brown-skinned woman. Angel thought she seemed pretty nice. Of course, she looked older, Angel thought. Angel thought all the women Brian was messing with looked older than her, but she was way older than them. Angel and Amy decided to do lunch. Angel was starving, they had agreed and decided to take Angel's car. Brian finally got in touch with Angel. "Where are you? she asked. Brian said at the phone store because apparently Brian's phone had gotten shut off. Angel said okay, Brian asked if she could come and meet him. Angel told him that she had Amy in her car. Brian went off. He asked, "Why the fuck is she in your car? Why can't she drive her own car?" Angel said, "Brian, please, this is hard enough for me. Let me just tell her I have to meet you then I will come back." Brian agreed. Angel drove to an empty parking lot. Brian came and met her; Angel couldn't believe it. Brian looked like a homeless person. It was so awful to see him looking like that, she felt so sorry for him. Brian hugged Angel, he began to tell her about his phone being off and how his credit cards got mixed up, but Amy had already filled Angel in on how Sharon was paying all of Brian's bills, so Angel figured that Sharon got fed up and took Brian off her account. Brian really didn't want Angel to meet with Amy. Angel told him, "It is going to be okay. She can't tell me anymore than what she has already." Brian hugged Angel and asked her if she needed gas money. Angel told him no, that she was okay. Brian said he was going to his mother's house that he would call her later.

Brian was so pissed that Brett did what he did, but he couldn't be mad because he made the same mistake. Brian had sat in the office a little longer, so he could plan a honeymoon for Angel and him. He wanted to surprise Angel with a get away cabin trip and then take her on a cruise. He knew he had owed her those trips since day one. Brian needed to know what date Angel had set for their wedding, so he called Angel. "Hey baby, what you are doing?" Brian asked. "Nothing, just planning with Diamond and Marcy." "Oh yeah, how is that going?" "It's going great." "Did you get a date yet?" Brian asked. Angel hesitated and said, "Yes, but I wanted to make sure it would be okay with you." Brian said, "Baby, you know I don't care, it's what you want. Angel took a deep breath in, and she told Brian she wanted it to be on November 10th, the day his father was buried, so he could have a good memory of your father, but if it was not okay, she can change it. "No, baby, that is good. I like that," Brian said. "That is perfect. Angel smiled; she was happy the date was set. Now they could move on. Angel asked Brian how things went with Brett. "It went okay. It bothers me that I had to let him go, but he understood." "I know,

baby, it will be okay. Hopefully, he can find something else soon," Angel replied. "ok, well, I love you. I am about to go to the other locations. I will see you later," Brian said. "Love you too. Angel just smiles because one thing about Brian that sure hasn't changed; he doesn't like to be on the phone long.

Angel and Amy are talking about all this stuff that went down with Brian. Of course, it is the same stuff that Angel had already heard from Amy. Amy wanted to know what Brian thought of them meeting. Angel hated lying, and she hated being in the middle of all of this, but she felt she needed to because Amy was connecting to Angel, and that gave her a little peace to where she would not be so angry. Angel told Amy that he wasn't happy, but it is her choice. Angel told her that Brian and her really don't discuss her. "We are trying to work through our own stuff." The conversation went on to the point where Amy started crying and doing exactly what Brian said she would do; Angel was starting to wonder if what all Brian said was true because it sure seemed like it. Angel had to drink at least two beers to be able to get through the conversation. Amy would go back and forth about her and Brian's sex sessions, and about Kathy and Sharon, and then she would do that fake crying Brian said she does. Angel was just trying so hard to just listen and not think about Brian; he just looked so bad. Angel wanted to be with him, not at this table with crazy Amy. Angel was on her way home now, she was so happy to get that over with, but she was hurt from hearing all the stuff about Brian and Amy having sex. Now that she put a face with the person, it was really hard. Angel just wanted to run away somewhere; she didn't want to feel. She wanted her heart back from Brian. Brian texted Angel, "Please tell me when you get home, pleeeease," he said. Angel called Brian after she had taken a shower and got ready for bed. Brian asked her how it went, she told him that it went okay. "It was a little hard because she keeps wanting to talk about you two sex sessions." "Why the fuck she keeps bringing that up?" Brian said. "I guess that's because that's all we did." Angel didn't want to hear that because she just felt like she wasn't enough. Why couldn't Brian teach her how to love him? She was willing to learn, she told him she would try anything once. Angel was so hurt by Brian, but she never showed him that hurt. She just stayed strong because that is what that little girl always did. Angel prayed and continued to ask God to give her peace.

It's the New Year, and Angel wanted so much to spend it with Brian, but once again, her mind went to what was Brian doing. Was he with Kathy again? Angel didn't have anything against Kathy, but Amy hated her, Angel just wanted to understand Brian. Angel was going to go out, but it was raining, so she just stayed in. She didn't even stay awake to bring in the New Year. She just slept her worries and pain away. Angel texted Brian's children and his mother to wish them a happy New Year. Brian once again did absolutely nothing. Angel was beginning to feel stupid. How could Brian love her or how could she be so special to him if he doesn't call her? Angel was playing tug-o-war with her emotions; she just wanted to have a holiday or something. Angel sat around the house, and of course, she got the text from Amy. It was a picture of Brian and Kathy at some party. This is really the first time Angel has seen Kathy's entire body, and wow, she is really not in shape, but it doesn't matter, she is with Brian. Brian really didn't look happy in the picture Angel thought, but she probably didn't want him to look happy. Later that night, Amy had sent Angel three pictures of Kathy and Brian. She had pasted on a picture of a walrus because Kathy had on a grey tight dress that was way too small for her, and she was shaped like a walrus. Angel couldn't help it; she was cracking up. Then the other picture was of a big white woman in a two piece on a beach. Amy captioned the picture: "well damn" with laughing emojis. It was funny, Angel thought. Amy texted

Angel and told her she sent that to Brian. Angel shook her head; she wonders what Brian did. Angel was kind of happy that Amy did that, and once again she felt that evil spirit start to come. Angel got off the phone with Amy and immediately started praying. Angel just wanted to be free from all of this. *God, just please hear me, fall fresh*. Angel asked God to forgive her for laughing at the picture, but Amy is crazy she thought. Angel just wanted God to heal her broken heart and just take Brian away or bring him back to her. Angel hated feeling like this. She always thinks she is getting better then something happens and reminds her, *Nope, you're still fucked up.* Angel just continues to pray; it is all she could do to keep from crying. *God, please, I give you all of me.* Angel is on her knees, crying out to God to remove, rebuild, and restore her. Angel has finally taken her hands off of Brian, she is giving him to God.

CHAPTER 9:

THE RELEASE

Angel goes back to planning. Now that she can set the date, she can move forward with the invitations and locations. Angel asked Diamond and Marcy, "Is this really going to happen? I'm finally going to be Mrs. Ward." Tears are falling from Angel's eyes, she remembers all the heartache she went through, but she refused to give up on her and Brian. God told her that Brian was the one. She just had to be patient while he breaks him down to get him ready. Diamond and Marcy just hug Angel and say yes, it's finally happening. Diamond said, "If he doesn't marry you, I'm going to kick Brian's ass!" They all laugh. They start wrapping things up because it's getting late. Angel hasn't cooked anything, and Brian will be home soon. Diamond and Marcy leave. Brian calls Angel to tell her he is on his way home, but he wanted her to get dressed up. He was taking her out for dinner. Angel was happy about that because she didn't want to cook. Brian took Angel to a very nice upscale restaurant. Angel asked him what the occasion was. "Why do I need one to take my soon to be wife out for dinner? Angel smiled. "No, you don't, but trust and believe when I become your wife you better not stop spoiling me." Brian smiles and says, I promise I will forever spoil you and love you. You are my queen." Angel thought Brian always did have a way with words. She would just melt.

"Did you get registered for school yet Matthew?" Angel asked. "No, not yet. I'm about to." Angel knew what that "I'm about to" meant, that his ass was going to forget. Matthew would forget his head if it weren't attached to him, but Angel loved him so much. He made her laugh. Hell, all her children made her laugh. Mary was sharp with her tongue, and very smart the only girl the boys spoiled her, and Angel did too maybe too much. Johnathan and Matthew were the same really just quite but if they got mad it was over, but They were all crazy and unique. She loved them all very much. Angel remembers all the laughs she had with Johnathan, and it brought tears of joy to her eyes. Mary called Angel; she wanted to take her out to dinner. Mary was going through her own heartache too with her boyfriend, so Angel and Mary would help each other get through their heartache. Sometimes it was just a train wreck, two broken hearted people trying to fix or help the other. That shit would work sometimes, but other times they were at each other's throat. Angel loved her, but thank God there was only one Mary she thought. Angel gets dressed. She and Mary love oysters, so they went to Bristol's. Mary loves that place. Angel had two beers and some oysters. Mary had her beer, a mixed drink, and oysters, they were having a good time. Mary drops Angel back at home, Angel is feeling relaxed and ready to unwind. Matthew comes in and asks where his food is at. Angel said, "In my belly. I am about to shit it out. You want it?" Matthew ran over to her and grabbed her. Matthew and Angel laughed. Angel gets in the shower. She always puts her worship music on, so she can release any negative energy. Angel gets in bed and meditates. She reads her Bible, and then she prays. Angel wakes up, meditates, prays, and does her worship music as she gets ready for work. She wants to stay in peace, no negative energy. Amy has calmed down, a lot so that is good. Angel hasn't heard that much from Brian, but she was just staying focused on her relationship with God, so she can release all that poison that is in her body, mind, and spirit. Angel is at the gym working out, and a guy comes up to her and her brother and introduces himself. Angel has seen him around the gym when she and Ralph would come to the gym. "What's up? My name is Tony." He starts asking Ralph questions about working out, and Angel is just doing her routine that Ralph has her doing. Tony was a nice-looking man Angel thought, but she had Brian on her mind, so she continued to work out while her brother ran his mouth. Tony and Ralph were talking for a while, and finally they got finished talking. Ralph and Angel finish their workout and head home. Angel asked Ralph, "What were you and that guy talking about?" Ralph told her that Tony thought they were married. Angel laughed, she said, "What did you tell him?" "I told him no, that you were my sister. He thought you were young." Angel is used to people thinking she is young, and it made her feel good sometimes. Ralph said, "Tony wants your number." "Really?" Angel was shocked. She hasn't been hit on for a minute. She was flattered. Ralph dropped Angel off at her condo, Angel went in, showered, and got ready for bed. She still was thinking about Tony wanting her number. She wasn't sure she wanted to give him her number. She was afraid, and she still loved Brian. Angel was mad at Brian for putting her in this situation, that she had to move on. She loved him, but she was hurt that Brian had moved on, so maybe it was time for her to do the same. Angel does her normal routine: meditate, pray, and read the Bible before she goes to sleep. Angel got up feeling good, she is doing her praise and worship as she is getting ready for work. Angel will not answer her phone while she is meditating or praying because she devotes an hour or two to God. Angel had decided to stay off all of social media until God released her. Angel can feel herself getting stronger, she was finally getting peace. She thanked God. Angel goes to work, does her normal lunch routine, praying asking God to restore, remove, and rebuild. Angel had no idea what that really meant, but she felt the need to pray for it along with peace. Angel would pray for everyone to have peace, for the hate to go away, and for people to release and give all their cares to God.

Angel is heading home from work. She hurries up and runs in to get dressed for the gym. Ralph is on the way to pick her up. Angel still didn't have a car yet. She either drives a rental or drives Matthew's dope mobile that she hated. Matthew had gotten so high one day that he came home. The entire passenger side tire had exploded, and the front bumper was hanging off. The car looked like someone took a huge can opener and started to open the car up on the side panel. Matthew had no clue what happened; he didn't know anything until he pulled the car up to Angel's apartment. Matthew walked in the house high as hell, telling Angel, "Now don't get mad, but I sort of messed up the car." Angel knew it was messed up bad. She walked outside, and the car looked like shit. She asked Matthew what happened, he said he didn't know, that he just remembered something being in the road. He saw the other cars running it over, so he went over it too. "There is no damn way you cause all of that damage from running over something in the road." By this time Ralph had pulled up and said that someone must have had an accident because there were car parts in the road up the street. Angel told Ralph, "It was jackass right here." Matthew was too high to even know what the hell was going on. Angel wanted to beat him. So, Ralph and Angel changed the tire. She tried to get Matthew to help, but he was just in the wind gone. He was singing, "Don't worry, be happy." Angel had to laugh. *This boy, I tell you*, she thought. Once she and Ralph get the tire changed out, they look over, and Matthew is on the little kids swing set just swinging. Angel records him, so when he sobers up, she is going to show him how he was acting, she sent to video to his sister and brother they all laughed. Angel can't wait for her insurance company to finally close the case, so she can get her vehicle she wants. Ralph and Angel head out to the gym. Ralph asked Angel if she is going to give Tony her number. Angel really doesn't know, her; heart is with Brian. They enter the gym, and Tony is standing over by the leg press. Angel thought, *Okay, you can do this. Fuck Brian! He is not thinking about you. Hell, he hasn't thought about you for a long time, up there fucking all these women.* Angel is still hurting over the fact he chose Amy over her. Ralph and Angel start their workout, and Tony heads their way. Of course, Ralph and Tony go on and on, and Tony looks at Angel. "Ralph is working you hard." Angel smiles. "Yes, he is, he is always working me hard." Ralph jumps in, "You want your body to look right, don't you?" "Yes," Angel answered with a smile. Tony starts making small talk with Angel, but he didn't want to interfere with her workout or his either, so he left them alone but would come over and make small talk with Ralph and her. They finish their workout. Tony rushes over. "Hey Angel, would it be okay if I get your number and call you sometime." Angel was blushing. She smiled and said yes, she gave him her number. Ralph joked with Angel the entire time on the way home. "Girl, Brian is going to kill you." "Fuck Brian. He can kill himself. He left me for a woman he can fuck in every hole." Angel couldn't get those words out of her head. Amy would say that all the time. He put his dick in every hole. Angel wanted to say, "That's because you were a hoe." She was getting angry. Angel realized that she hadn't really forgave Brian even though she was helping him and trying to be there for him. She still had her own healing she had to do. She had to be released. She didn't know that she was bitter and angry; she knew the hurt, pain. *Ok, Angel get yourself together. No negative energy.* Angel runs upstairs to her condo. Matthew is in the kitchen looking for food. "Mama!" he yells. "What you cooking?" "Nothing." Angel laughs. "No, I don't know yet. What do you want? Matthew always wants rice. So, he said rice and chicken. Angel takes her shower and starts dinner, her phone rings. It's a text. "Hello, beautiful. This is Tony. How are you doing? Would it be okay if I call you now?" Angel was smiling from him calling her beautiful. She remembers when Brian would always text her or call her that. "Give me a minute. I am cooking," Angel texted back. "Ok," replied Tony. Angel was so nervous. She hasn't had a real conversation with a man for a while now, she really can't say she and Brian really had any good conversation since the HIV and his father's death. Angel gets in her bed. "I'm free now," she texted Tony. Her phone immediately rings. "Hello beautiful," Tony replies. "Hello, sir." The conversation between the two lasts for two and half hours. Angel can't remember when the last time she was on the phone that long with Brian, it felt good to hear a man's voice and to feel appreciated and wanted. *This feels nice,* Angel thought. Angel did her normal routine: meditated, prayed, and read the Bible. Angel still longed for Brian; she couldn't help it. *What the fuck did this man do me? Is it true? "Did he breathe something in me? Did he possess me with his spirit?* Angel was questioning everything because she wanted to not care, but she couldn't. She could still feel him inside of her. *Father, God, release all of this negative energy. Fill me with your love, grace, and mercy. Give me peace tonight. Amen.*

Brian pays for the meal, they head home. Angel asked Brian, "Are you okay? "Yes, baby, I am." Brian kisses her. "No need to worry. Angel knows this Brett thing is bothering Brian. It makes him think back to the past. Angel asked Brian, "So, what are we doing for our honeymoon? Brian smiles. You let me worry about that." "OK, daddy, you going to surprise mommy?" Angel loves when Brian surprises her. It is always amazing to her. Brian told her, "You just pack something sexy, no sweatpants." "Shut up." Angel and Brian laugh. They make it home. Both Angel and Brian are exhausted. They get undressed and lay down for the night. Angel loves it more just having Brian hold her through the night. She loves when he rolls over like he is looking for her to hold her. She becomes his

security blanket. "Night baby," says Brian. "Goodnight, love," Angel tells him.

Angel wakes up, feeling like she has been hit by a truck. She immediately starts her morning meditation and prayer. Angel gets a good morning text from Tony. "Morning beautiful. I hope you have a wonderful day. Call me when you get a break." Angel smiles but wishes it was from Brian. Oh well, she thought, she is going to try to make this work. Brian has moved on, so it is time she did too. Angel gets dressed for work. She has a very busy day. Her schedule is booked with patients and meetings. Angel is everywhere at work. She finally is able to take a lunch. She goes and clears her head to get ready for the next couple of hours. Angel wonders what Brian is doing. *Does he even think about me? God*, she asks, *please God, I just need a sign. Something to let me know what to do.* Just then Tony sends a text. "Hello, beautiful. I was thinking about you." *OK, God, you are being funny*, Angel thought. *Is this what you trying to tell me, to move on?* It really didn't matter at that time what sign God gave her. Angel's heart was with Brian. Angel calls Tony. "Hello, how are you?" "I am good and you?" "I am good, just got a chance to take a break." "You been busy today?" "Yes, it is a madhouse today. Everyone is sick, and with the COVID-19, it doesn't help out either." "That is just sad, but you stay safe. I don't want nothing to happen to you before I could get a chance to spoil you." Angel just smiles as she blushes. She hasn't been spoiled for a while now. "I would love that." "So how about dinner tonight?" Angel's heart sank. She doesn't know if she is ready for that. "Umm, OK, what time?" "How about 8:00?" "That should be fine." "It's a date. See you then beautiful." Angel gets off the phone, she doesn't know how to feel. She is happy to have someone interested in her, but at the same time, she longed for Brian, and not to mention, she had this sickness in her that she didn't know how she was going to tell Tony if things worked out for them. The day drags on. Angel is ready to go home, shower, and get dressed up. She hasn't dressed up for a while.

Angel is home. Finally, she thought, *what a day*. She jumps in the shower to hurry to get ready, she sends Tony her location. Angel gets out of the shower. She sees her phone ringing. It's Brian. *Oh, my God, does he know? He can't be feeling my energy.* "Hello." "Hey, baby." Angel didn't know what to say to that. "Yes. You okay? "Yes, I just need to get help. It's time. Do you have anyone I can go see? How about your therapist? Angel was for sure not sending him to hers. He would probably end up fucking her, but Angel did have one for Brian. She has been holding onto this information, waiting for the right time, and now it is the right time. Angel gives Brian the name and address to a male therapist. Her doctor said he is really good. Brian didn't sound like himself; he sounded really down. Angel didn't know what was going on. They talked for a little bit. Brian was at work, so he didn't have that much time. Even if he did, he wasn't going to talk long with Angel. Angel continues to get dressed. She tried to stay focused with positive energy. Angel hears a knock at the door, she opens it. "WOW look at you! You are so beautiful." Angel smiles. "Thank you, you look good too." Tony actually looked very good. He was filling out that button up shirt, his jeans fit really nice, and he was very clean. Angel started to feel that little girl in her try to come out, she was so scared. Angel just took a deep breath and grabbed her jacket and out they went. Tony drove a BMW X7. It was very sexy, Angel thought. Tony took Angel to this very nice restaurant. Tony knew Angel loved seafood from their conversation. Angel was impressed. Tony opened Angel's door and grabbed her hand. Angel didn't know what to feel. She just felt that little girl, she took another deep breath, tried to release all her fears. The conversation with Tony was what Angel needed; she felt important. He was asking her opinion on things, getting to know more about her. Tony was sharing himself, something Brian rarely did. It was like pulling teeth to get anything out of him, probably because he was lying so much. He didn't want the lies to come out. Angel was a great listener; the night went on, and they ate and talked, it was going really well. Tony walks Angel to her door. "I had a great time." "Me too." "I hope to see you again." "That would be nice." Angel can feel her heart racing from the fear of him wanting to kiss her. Tony leans over toward Angel and tries to kiss her. Angel pulls away. "I can't right now. Please understand." "I can wait. You are worth it, and I understand." "Thank you for a wonderful night, Tony. "No, thank you, Ms. Angel, for giving your time to share it with me." Angel walks in, and who is there waiting? Matthew, yes. "Who was that?" "Just a friend." "Oh, OK, friend." "Boy, move." "You bring any food back?" "In fact, I did. Here. Now, leave me alone." Angel goes to her room. She is so tired from work. She gets undressed, meditates, and prays. *Father, please help me to understand what it is you are doing. Why do I continue to long for this man when clearly, he doesn't want to have nothing to do with me? Am I stupid for even believing there will be a us, a we?* Angel starts crying. *Father, I can't keep doing this. I'm so weak, and my heart is so heavy with grief from wanting him. Please take away this feeling. If it's lust or longing, I don't want it. Just remove it. Let me release all that is not pleasing to you, father. I just need a sign from you.* Angel cries herself to sleep.

Brian wakes up first. He kisses Angel on her forehead. "Good morning, baby." "Morning love." Brian goes and takes a shower; Angel stays in the bed; she doesn't want to get up. Brian goes downstairs and attempts to try to make breakfast for Angel. Angel goes back to sleep. She is dreaming of becoming Mrs. Ward. Brian comes upstairs with the tray of food. He made her some eggs and bacon with some fruit. "Baby, baby, Mrs. Ward." Angel wakes up and sees Brian smiling with the tray of food. Angel just smiles. "Aww, baby, you cooked." Angel felt like the luckiest woman in the world. She knows it is not always going to be perfect between her and Brian, but they both agreed that they will always communicate with each other and try not to go to bed angry. Brian leaves for his meetings and makes his rounds. Angel just lays around. She is off today, so she just wants to be lazy... She thought, *I am not even going to do any of the wedding* planning. I *just want to lay in bed and feel at peace.*

The next day, Angel's eyes were puffy from crying, but she felt like she had released some of the stuff that was eating away at her. She knew she needed to talk to Brian in order for her to have a better understanding of things. Brian has been dodging her, he barely talks to her. Angel was always too afraid of the truth to even ask him questions. All of this holding everything in was killing her. Angel got dressed and headed out; she had to meet with her therapist. Angel had released a mouthful on her therapist; she told her about the date with Tony, how he tried to kiss her, and she couldn't do it. She explains her emotions, her therapist agreed with her that it was time to have a talk with Brian, and it needed to be face to face. Brian would always want to talk over the phone, and then he would say, "Oh, I got to go." Angel always felt like she had to rush to get everything out. She could never remember everything; she knew Brian was just running. That is what he is good at, sometimes he doesn't even know he is doing it until Angel tells him. That night Angel sent Brian a text. "Hey Brian, I hope you are well; I was wondering if you could please find time to have a sit down with me. I really need to talk to you. I need to be able to move on, like you have, so you owe me this. I went on a date, and I couldn't even let the guy kiss me. This is killing me, so please, Brian, no more running." Brian texted her back. "I will make that happen; I promise." Angel gave a day, and Brian agreed to it. He said he had therapy that day, so it works, that he can come after. Brian had shared his first session with Angel. She was blown away; she never thought he would go; she was very happy. The next day Brian had sent Angel a happy Tuesday text. He told her he was getting more clients. Angel told him that is great. Brian said he was praying and meditating more, Angel was really impressed with Brian praying. Angel had sent Brian this sermon. It was a very powerful one. Once the pastor was done preaching at the end, he would say if you wanted God, you need to humble yourself. Fall on your knees and ask God to enter you. Give yourself to God. Angel had prayed one night, asking God to give her a sign. She told Him if Brian is not the man for her, take him away, but if he is the man, make him bow down and confess God as his lord and savior. Angel figured God was surely going to take Brian away from her because there was no way in hell that man would ever bow down to God. So, Angel sent the sermon to him anyway. Brian was just talking about how he lights candles and sage to remove the evil spirits, really to remove all those females he had over his house fucking Angel thought. Angel told Brian, "OK, now you need to purge." Brian asked her what that was, she told him to ask God to release all that yucky stuff that is in him. Brian said, "I already did. When you sent me that sermon, I did what the man told me. I got on my knees and asked God to help me." Angel just cried. She was shaking because she just witnessed a miracle. It truly blew her mind. Brian said, "Angel I'm not lying. I felt God move in me." Angel just had no words; she knew that was her confirmation that God was getting Brian right, and he saved him. Brian was able to release all that stuff in him and give it to God.

That night, God told Angel to write Brian a letter. Angel was so worried about her and Brian's meeting she didn't want to forget anything. God said just write it down. Angel sat at the computer typing away. When she was finished, it was 7 pages long. *OK, God, Brian is not going to sit and listen to all of this.* Brian barely read anything Angel wrote; he always complained. God said yes, he will. Angel prayed over the letter and went to bed. She meditated, prayed, and read her Bible. Angel was trying to take her mind off of seeing Brian. It has been about a month now since she last saw him. Angel awakes. She gets in the shower and prays, asking God to allow Brian to feel, hear, and understand. She prayed for peace. Angel is so nervous. Brian knocks at the door, "Hey." "Hello." Brian reaches to hug Angel. "I can't hug you because my flesh is weak." Angel takes Brian in the bedroom. "Why are we going in the bedroom?" "Just sit down, and I don't know when Matthew was going to come back, so just chill. It's alright. I have something I need to read to you. It's a bit long." "Oh no, can I have some tissues?" Brian asked. Angel gave Brian a tissue, and she proceeded to read the letter. Brian was crying. Angel was crying because Angel was finally able to release some of the hurt that Brian had caused her. Brian was able to hear what he was running from and release what kept him in the dark to cause Angel and other people pain. Brian had grabbed Angel's hand once she was finished reading. He prayed for that little hurt girl and the hurt little boy. Brian had been molested by a male and a female; one was a family member. Brian finally heard Angel's story. He never knew about the hurt little girl nor her struggle; he was full of tears and regret for adding to her pain. Angel was able to tell Brian how much she hurt over him doing all of this to her. He didn't appreciate, value, or respect her. "You made me believe I was the problem!" Angel yelled. "You treated me so bad." Brian said, "I know, and I'm so sorry." "Why Brian? You made me feel so nasty. Was it because I didn't know much about sex? Is that why you left me for Amy?" "No, baby, no. "Can't you see you are a lady? You are a fucking lady. Amy is... she is nothing to me. I had everything with you. I was just scared, and I didn't think I was good enough for you. You intimidated me to the point to cause me to run.

I knew I hurt you so bad with the lies, that I couldn't face you, nor could I hear your voice." "I just don't understand, Brian." "Baby, I was sick. Well, I am sick. I was hurting, and hurt people hurt people. It was like I was a person on drugs. When they get help, they realize they did a lot of shit to hurt people. When they were high, they had no clue. I was sick. My therapist asked me why I needed all those women. I told him I didn't know. I could have just been with you. Angel, you were everything. I need to heal; you need to heal. Who knows what may come, but I have a lot of healing I have to do?" They both cried some more and agreed on the healing. Angel knew it was going to be hard. Even though she had released, she still longed for him, but she knew it was going to take time for her to forgive him, and it was going to take time for Brian to forgive himself. "Whatever you do, Angel, don't change. Don't let anyone change you. You are a gift. You are truly an angel. You don't know how powerful you are. You will always be very special to me; we are more than friends. When I make it, you will never have to want for anything financially. I will give you everything." Angel loved to hear that, but her heart didn't care about the money. She just wanted to build with him, be one, and grow together. Brian hugged Angel and said goodbye. Angel still held onto what God promised. The first will be last, and the last will be first. Trust the process. Angel felt a little better, but she always feels like she should have said more. She thinks it's because she is so busy thinking if only, she did or said this, Brian would come running to her. It's time she trusts God and let him do what he does. She is not ready for Brian, and Brian is not ready for anyone now. God said whoever gets Brian now will not end up with him, so if you want him now, just know it will not last in the long run. Angel just cried. *Thank you, Father, for the release and for freeing us both, for giving* confirmation *and allowing me to witness your miracle with Brian. I would go through it all over again if it meant it would save his soul. You are an amazing God; I will always honor and adore you. Amen.*

CHAPTER 10:

SURRENDERING TO FORGIVENESS

It is getting closer to the wedding date, and Angel is on pins and needles. She is driving Diamond and Marcy crazy. "Girl, if you don't settle down, me and Marcy are going to lock your ass up in the damn closet with your damn self. Your doing too much." Diamond was done. "OK, OK, I just can't believe in 2 days I will be Mrs. Ward. It's happening, but what if he changes his mind?" "Girl, if you don't get that negative energy out your head... Here, let's drink some wine." Marcy always believed wine can fix anything, and it did. Angel was finally relaxing. Angel had to do her final fitting for the dress, so they all go to the bridal shop. Marcy has always been right by Angel's side through everything. They have been close for over 20+ years. Marcy was dating Ralph Angel's brother for years and gave him 4 children, she put up with his shit for 20 years. Ralph never married her, it broke Marcy really bad. Ralph would verbally and mentally abuse her to the point Marcy lost herself. She gave up, so she settled for

Ralph's BS. Angel would try to tell her to leave him, but love will have you do whatever. Angel could only be there for her because she knew just because she was tired, Marcy had to be tired for herself. When the heart wants what the heart wants there is nothing nobody can say or do you have to go through it yourself. Ralph ended up marring some young girl, who ended up treating him like he treated Marcy, and their marriage didn't even last a year. Now Ralph is heartbroken. Marcy forgave Ralph for the hurt he caused, but Ralph denies he caused her any pain.

Brian calls while they are at the shop. "Hello, Mrs. Ward, how are you?" Angel is in tears with her emotions. She is driving Marcy and Diamond crazy to the point they are yelling through the phone "Brian come and get her ass. She just keeps crying. If she is not crying, she is yelling at us. Come get her." Brian starts laughing. "Baby, you being bad? Angel smiles and says, "Yes, I just can't believe this is going to happen." "Believe it baby! It is. I love you. I will see you when I get home and stop being difficult, ok. Angel smiled. "Love you." Love you too." "Mmhmm, that's all it took is for Brian to call your cry baby ass for you to smile," Diamond said. They all laughed; Angel went back to put on her dress. It fit perfect; it was so beautiful that Angel started crying again. "Oh, lord, here we go again." Marcy said, "Girl, you going to have us crying." They all were crying by this time. They finished there and went to do makeup and get a spa treatment Angel was treating them, she wanted to surprise them. Marcy and Diamond enjoyed their treatment. They then headed out for lunch, to go over everything to make sure they had everything covered for November 10. What Angel didn't know is that Mary and Marcy had planned a lady's night out. Since Mary was more outgoing, she knew of all the good places to have the bachelorette party.

After the meeting with Brian, Angel felt a little better, but she still missed him she longed to be with him. Angel was determined to follow God's plan, to just keep pushing through it all. Angel knew deep down inside she wasn't really ready to be with Brian because she hasn't forgiven him yet. *This is so hard*, Angel thought. *How in the fuck do I still love this man? He has shitted on me, and even he said it. What is wrong with me?* Angel thought, *oh my God, I must be really stupid.* Angel immediately started meditating and praying to get rid of all that doubt. She needed to heal, she needed to surrender herself to God, so he could allow her to forgive Brian completely. The days went on. It wasn't easy. Angel just tried to put herself into her work and doing other things: working out, praying every day and night. Mediating, trying not to think negative and think about Brian, which was hard. Angel thought about Brian every day, but she pushed through it. Angel had to tell Tony she couldn't date him, not now because she needed to heal first to see what God has for her. Tony asked if he still could be her friend just to go out from time to time. Angel agreed that it would be fine, but she just didn't want to rush into anything. The days go by, and Angel is still longing for Brian. She gets mad when she starts thinking about everything, how Brian didn't take her to the cabins, and the sex with Amy really bothered her. She couldn't get past that he was blowing her off to spend time with Amy, who is clearly crazy. Angel realized that she still hasn't forgiven him because it still hurts to think of all the lies. How he was in a whole fucking relationship with Sharon all this time, how he mistaken and texted her instead of Sharon and said, "I love you Mrs. Brown". That really hurt Angel. Brian just lies one after another. Angel knew that she needed to heal, that it was a good thing. Well, Amy has found something to entertain her for the time being. She started getting involved in all these chat rooms, she would spend hours in these different rooms. Amy called Angel to share an idea she had. She was thinking about creating her own chat room, she needed a name, so Angel helped her with a name. Then, Amy wanted her to join the group. Angel really doesn't have time like Amy does. Amy doesn't have a job; she has a nonprofit she runs, but she helps her sister out with her business. Angel decides to join the group just to please Amy, so she would stay busy. She knows Brian really doesn't want her interacting with Amy, but Angel believes everything happens for a reason, and she just cannot hate people. everyone deserves forgiveness. Amy still hasn't accepted Brian's apology because she doesn't believe he has changed.

Brian has not called or text. Angel really didn't think he was going to, but she just was hoping he did. Angel just kept pushing through the days. Trusting God that he will make a way. Angel finally got her new car; she had been waiting patiently for about 8 months now. Angel was so tired of driving Matthew's dope mobile; and renting cars, she was able to get the car she wanted. Angel had told Brian she would show him the car when she got it, she wanted to surprise him. Brian told her he couldn't wait to see it. Angel had a meeting she was scheduled for in two days. She had her appointment with her doctor for her 6-month checkup. Angel decided she will also stop by Brian's job to show him her new baby. Precious, that is what she named her car.

Angel really just wanted to see Brian, just to see if he was okay. Angel is at work. It is a busy day. A lot of people are coming in with fevers. She is afraid she may contract COVID from one of the patients she is seeing. She makes sure she is being very cautious, considering her situation. She doesn't want to get sick. So many people are dying because of this damn COVID. It hurts Angel so much to have to tell her patients' family that their loved one is not going to make it and to prepare for the worst. Angel thinks about Brian that last time she saw him. He looked bad. She worried about his health, but she knew there was nothing she could do. This is a path of healing Brian had to go on his own. Angel felt she had done her part. Now he has to surrender to God, so he can have forgiveness. Angel gets home, she gets ready for the gym. She knows that Tony is going to be there. She likes the fact that she gets some male attention, and it makes her feel a little better about herself. Tony doesn't mind giving her all his attention. Tony still calls her, he tries to be patient with Angel, but he is a man with needs Angel thought, but she just is not ready to go down that road. "Hello, beautiful," Tony greets Angel at the gym. "Hello, Tony, how are you doing?" "I am fine now that my Queen is here." Angel smiled. If Tony only knew that Angel was thinking, *I wish this were Brian saying that.* Of course,

Ralph could spoil a wet dream with his silly self. He always got something nasty and smart to say. "I bet you just nutted all over yourself," Ralph said to Tony. "Ah, man, come on now. Why you go say that?" Angel just walked away. Ralph and Angel did their workout. Ralph was always talking loudly, so everyone in the gym could hear him torturing Angel on whatever he had her working on that day. Angel hated leg day. It was awful, but she loved the results. Tony would come over and flirt a little with Angel, and of course she didn't mind because she likes the attention, he was giving her. Angel got home and jumped right into the shower; she was so tired. Tomorrow she will see Brian, and hopefully it will be a good visit. Angel prayed, meditated, and read her Bible. Angel didn't sleep well last night. She had Brian on her mind, she was so nervous in seeing him, wondering if he was going to be there, if he would be mad for her just showing up. So many things ran through her mind. It was driving her crazy. Angel got up, did her meditation, prayed and got dressed, then she headed out to her meeting and then to her doctor's appointment. Her appointment went well, and her test results were good, so she was happy about that. Angel wondered a lot about Brian's health. Is he *still good? What is going on with him?* Brian never really talked to Angel about that stuff. He did in the beginning but lately nothing. *I just wished Brian would talk to me, tell me what he is feeling, what he is going through, but he just holds everything in.* Angel was thinking to herself. Angel leaves her doctor's office. She is on her way to Brian's job. She can feel the butterflies in her stomach as she pulls up to his job. She drives to the back because she didn't want Amy to see her. She goes and knocks on the door. "Hey, baby!" Brian says with a surprised look on his face. "Hey, I gave birth. Precious is finally here," said Angel. Brian walks out to see Angel's car. It is an all-black Lexus 2022. "Aww, baby this is nice. This is really nice. When did you get it?" "Saturday." "Wow, it really fits you, your personality." "Thank you. Hey, do you mind if I go in and change my clothes?" Angel wanted to change into her workout clothes because she was going straight to the gym. "No, come on in. You can use my office, OK?". Angel walks in the gym. Brian had two older ladies he was training. "Hello ladies," Angel said. "He is not working you too hard, is he?" The ladies moan and laugh. "Yes, he is." Angel goes to Brian's office and changes. She comes out and gives Brian a bag of clothes she had brought for the twins. "Thanks baby." "Ok, well I'm going to go." "ok, baby, I love you." "Love you too. Let me know when you make it home." Angel wasn't for sure what to feel about Brian calling her baby and saying he loved her. She thought, *is that something he just says to everyone he had a relationship with? Did it mean anything to him? The words I love you.* She drove away. Brian still looked bad, she just worried about him so much, but she kept telling herself, *It is not for you to fix. You can't fix it. You need to focus on you. This man hurt you, and you can't trust him.* Angel knew the hurt she felt was so deep, that she tries not to think about the lies and the women. It made her too sad. Angel just focuses on what she and Brian used to have, the joy, laughter, and the togetherness. Angel wishes she knew what was going on in Brian's head. He seems like he just shut the entire world out. Angel is heading home now; she feels a little down because she knows she has to walk away from Brian now and heal herself. She has been so focused on Brian and his healing that she hasn't healed. Angel showers, she starts praying in the shower because she knows this is it, that this may have been the last time she saw or heard from Brian. She has to surrender all of herself to healing and forgiving Him. Angel can feel the pain all over again, she realizes all this time she was so focused on helping Brian and trying to prevent Amy from reporting Brian that she hid her own pain because she didn't want to feel the pain Brian had caused her because if she did, she might just hate him. Angel realized that she really did hurt. She had nothing left to give, she was empty. All she could do is ask God to forgive her for feeling the hate inside of her that was growing. The tears began to fall as she finally surrenders to what she was hiding all this time, her pain. Angel hates to feel pain. She always tries to run from it, so she reached out to Brian's son Jeff first to see if he wanted to finally have dinner. He and his girlfriend couldn't, and then she reached out to his mother to see if she wanted to get together, but she also couldn't. Angel knew God was keeping her still, so she can finally feel the pain and grow from it, so she can finally forgive. She had to endure for her to be able to surrender to the hurt. Being treated like shit, lied to, cheated on, and not valued for her worth, she had to see all of those things and felt what she hated to feel that made her weak. She knew God had his hands on her. She couldn't run anymore. She had to face her fears and accept what had happened. She had to accept that she is HIV positive, and the man she loves may not love her anymore. Angel had to accept that she cannot help nor give any more time or energy to Brian because he is on his own journey. Angel had to finally surrender, so she can fully forgive Brian. Tears filled her pillow as she prayed.

Mary comes over to Angel's house to pick her up to head to the secret location that she had planned for Angel's Bachelorette Party. Diamond and Marcy are already there, making sure everything is set up, they are greeting the guest.

"Bye, babe," Brian calls to Angel.

"Be good."

"I will. You better be good."

Brian was going to his bachelor party with his boys. They both head out. Mary and Angel talk in the car about some of the past.

Mary said, "Mom, I remember when you were crying and praying about marrying Brian. I really didn't believe it was going to happen because of all this time that had went by."

"Yes, I know, but God told me. I just can't explain it, God just kept telling me to be patient. I just didn't know it was going to take 2 years, but it needed to because Brian appreciates me more. We communicate better, and it gets better each day, especially now that he is going to therapy."

Mary said, "I can tell. You look so happy. I prayed he did right by you finally."

They both laughed. Mary pulls up to the club.

"Oh, now what in the hell have you brought me to?" Mary just smiles.

"You will see. You will have fun."

Angel walks in and sees Marcy running up to her with this sash saying Bride to Be. Then Diamond ran up to her with a crown. Angel was in tears with joy. People from her work had come and other people. Her sisters and mother were there. Elizabeth was there, her and Angel have become good friends by now. Karen and Janae' came as well. She was so happy. Angel can't remember the last time she had gone out and danced her butt off. She was enjoying the moment. Seeing everyone around her have a great time just made her feel that this is perfect, they did good.

Brian and his boys were at a strip club (go figure). They would take him there, but Angel had already known she trusted Brian. She remembers when trust wasn't easy for her, but Brian has proven that he has left all that lying and cheating in the past. Brian enjoyed being with his boys and hanging out, but he did think about Angel. He knew that Mary really didn't care for him, so he wondered where she took Angel. Brian was still protective over Angel. His dick was the only dick he wanted Angel to see, he treated Angel like his little virgin girl because to him he was her first.

Brian couldn't resist, so he went to the bathroom and called Angel to see what he heard in the background. "Hey baby."

"Hey, love!"

"You having fun?"

"Oh, yes! Mary really got me."

"So, where she take you?"

"To some club, not sure."

"Are there any naked men there?"

Angel just laughed. "Why, do you want them to be?"

"Fuck no!" Brian said. "My dick is all you need."

Angel said, "You got that right, and it is all I can handle."

"That's right."

"You can't talk. I know your boy Derrick took you to a strip club because he likes shit like that, so what you looking at?"

"Babe, you already know I only want your good pussy, when you get home, I am going to give you this big, hard dick."

"Stop, you know how I get when you talk like that."
"What you getting wet aren't you?"

"Bye, Brian, love you."

"Love you too babe."

Angel and Brian get home only minutes apart. Brian grabs Angel.

"You ready for some of this dick, Ms. Ward."

"I have been ready."

"Oh, OK, you a big girl now, huh? We will see."

" You better not hurt me.'

Brian smiles. "Do I ever hurt you?" "Well." "No, no, don't answer that."

Just then Brian takes off Angel's clothes. He gets a blanket and lays It down. Brian takes off his clothes Angel still is impressed with the size of Brian's dick. She thinks it is just too big, but he makes it fit, it feels so good. Brian lays Angel down and slowly kisses her. He tells her over and over how much he loves her, how he wouldn't change one thing about her. Angel tells Brian how much she loves him, how he has always been so caring; she loves that he is so protective over her, she knows his heart is real, and she loves how he is so gentle with her. They make love, and it is truly amazing as it always is.

Today is the day. Angel leaves to head to the village suites where she is getting married. Marcy comes and picks her up, Derrick comes and gets Brian. Brian kisses Angel, "You're finally going to be my wife." Angel just started to cry. Brian whispers, "Babe, don't cry. It's a happy day." "Yes, it is a very happy day. Angel is in her room getting ready. Marcy is there with her.

"It's really happening."

"Yes, it is." "Oh, my God, I just can't believe this day would come. All the tears I cried over the years from the hurt the doubt, but I kept holding on to my faith."

"Yes, you did and look at you. You said God told you Brian was the one."

"Marcy, I can't even imagine this day being any perfect. I can't thank you and Diamond enough for putting up with me, for doing all of this."

Diamond had just come into the room. "They are about ready for you. Angel had put her dress on. Marcy and Diamond gushed.

"Aw, you look so beautiful." They all shed a couple of tears, they had to get their makeup touched up. Angel goes down a hallway where she is greeted by Matthew. He looked so handsome; he helps her get in the carriage. They ride to the location where they wait for the ceremony to start. Angel is so nervous.

"Matthew, you look so handsome."

"Yeah, yeah, I know. I got swag.

"Mom you look beautiful."

"Yeah, yeah, I know. I got swag."

They both laugh.

"But thank you, son.

"I know you have been waiting on this day forever."

"Yes, I have, and thanks to you, I was able to keep my strength. Thank you for holding me and comforting me when I was going through my storm."

The carriage starts to proceed down the roadway, they get to the front of the building where Timothy is waiting for her to walk her down the aisle. The music plays and everyone stands as Angel and Timothy proceed down the walkway, Timothy can't help it he is fighting back his tears.

"Mom you are so beautiful, and I am so happy to finally see you happy", Angel smiles and kisses Timothy on his cheek, "thank you I love you. "

They continue down the walkway, where Brian is waiting. Angel can see Brian through her veil, she can see the tears falling down his face. She is trying to hold back her tears, so she won't mess up her makeup. Angel makes it down to Brian, and they are looking each other in the

eye, both trying not to cry as the pastor announces them husband and wife. "You may kiss your bride." Brian had kissed Angel like she was going to leave him, but it felt so good Angel thought. Angel and Brian head over to the reception part where everything was set up. It looked amazing; it was exactly how Angel imagined it. The emerald green and gold, it was amazing. Everyone danced and ate. It was so nice. Angel's dream had come true. God kept his promise.

The days were long, but Angel knew she had to continue to press on. She held onto God's promise. She just kept praying. Brian didn't call or text her. Angel finally backed off, she continued to do her routine and stayed focused on healing herself. It has been a year since all of this stuff had happened. Some days are good, and some are bad, but Angel knows that the storm won't last forever. Angel continued to pray and held unto God's word. Angel knew she had to walk by faith not by sight because Brian was still entertaining Kathy and Sharon and whoever else. Angel just kept pressing on. She didn't do the social media. She just kept pushing, praying. Angel believed that Brian would be her husband, and it didn't matter what it looked like now; it's what happens at the end.

Angel is so excited to find out what Brian has planned for their honeymoon.

"Pack your bags, and don't worry about anything else. Make sure you have a couple of swimsuits."

Angel was just bouncing off the walls, trying to figure out what to pack for a vacation that she has no clue of where they are going.

"Ok, can I ask how long we will be gone?"

"2 weeks," Brian said.

"Well damn, that is a lot of packing for me to not know."

"I'm not telling you, babe. Just pack for every environment."

Angel got all packed. Brian got the truck all packed for the drive to the mountains. Angel had no clue. She just enjoyed the drive to just reflect on everything, how she is so happy right now being Mrs. Ward.

"So, you're not telling me anything."

"Nope, you will see."

"Ok, then, be that way." Angel was taking in the scenery of nature and how thankful she is that God showed favor on her. Angel knew it was God's grace that brought her through all of this and her faith that it all will work out. She knew that she had to eventually let go of the past, her hurt with her mother who caused the little girl in her to struggle with herself. Angel knew now that her mother also had her own issues she was dealing with. She was a mother at 16. What did she really know about being a mother? She did the best she knew how with what she had. She raised 5 children by herself, *I think we all came out damn good*, Angel thought as she looked back at the times, how they would make jokes, and how her brother Peter would make them race to take his shoes off for candy bars. *We had some good times*. Angel really missed Peter, but she knew her mother missed him more. Angel forgave her mother; she embraced the love she has now with her. Just like Brian, Angel was able to surrender to all that pain and embrace the new life that God gave her to be able to forgive is a blessing. She is very thankful for the storms because it gave her strength, a story. She is able to appreciate life more. Brian pulls up to this amazing cabin in the woods. It was so beautiful.

"Oh, my God! Brian, really!"

"Yes, babe, really! This is what I should have done for you a long time ago. You deserve it all, and if I could give you all that you desire, I would". Angel is crying.

"Babe, you have already made me the happiest woman in the world by giving me your last name and for honoring me. I love you so much, Brian."

Brian picks Angel up and carries her in the cabin. There are flowers everywhere. Angel remembers the first set of flowers Brian got her. No roses, they were wildflowers. He said those last longer and he wanted to be different. So, he had wildflowers and roses. There was wine and chocolate covered strawberries, Angel's favorite. Angel was just happy that Brian had planned all of this.

"We're going to be here for two weeks."

"No, babe just a week, and then I got another surprise for you."

Angel just felt like a little kid.

"Really! I can't wait! I mean, I can do the woods, but shoot, after a week, I am done with that."

Brian just laughed. "I know you are."

It felt good to finally have Brian know who I am really, Angel thought. He took the time to get to know the real Angel. Brian had a lot of activities set up for them. They went hiking and then on jet skis. Angel never rode on jet skis. She was so scared she rode on the back with Brian holding tight on his waist. She was so afraid. She just closed her eyes. *Lord, if you take me out now, and let the sharks eat me, I will be okay, at least I died happy*, she prayed. They went out to eat, did zipline, and of course made love just about everywhere. Angel was just so happy; she couldn't remember being this happy. Brian and Angel sat out in the jacuzzi to look out on nature they just enjoyed the peace that it brought.

"It is so beautiful out here. Thank you, baby. You really got me."

Brian was happy to be able to make Angel smile because he gave her so much pain back then, but he finally forgave himself, so he could love her again. He surrendered all that hurt that he inflicted on her and the hurt that was inflicted on that little boy. He has made peace, and he has forgiven, so he could be free. They spent the night out on the deck, laying out to watch the sunrise, and of course, Brian falls fast asleep. Angel just looks at him and thanks God for allowing them to find each other again.

They are off now to the other surprise Brian has for Angel. Angel can't wait. She had such a wonderful time in the cabins. What could out do that? Brian pulls up to the airport.

"Oh, we are flying this time?"

"Yes,

"this must be a faraway trip."

"Yes."

That is all she could get out of Brian. Brian wouldn't even let her see the ticket until they got inside the airport.

"Oh, we're going to Florida on the beach."

"Mmhh."

"Ok, Brian, I know you are lying. You only say 'mmhh' when you are telling a story."

"Well, stop asking me all these questions, so I won't have to lie to you."

Angel smiles. She never flew with Brian, so this is a first for him and her. She tries not to think about when he flew out with Kathy, but oh, well, she is his wife now, not Kathy or Amy, or Sharon. It was her. Brian grabs her hand and tells her to put all that negative energy away. Angel smiles and says okay. She hated how he could feel her energy. They board the plane. Angel fell asleep on Brian's shoulder. Brian kissed her forehead.

"Babe, we are here. Wake up."

Angel mumbled, "We're already here?"

"Yes, babe."

They get off the plane.

"Now what?

"You will see."

Brian goes get a shuttle.

"Aren't we going to get our bags?"

"No, we don't need to. They will bring them to us." Finally, the shuttle takes them to the dock where the cruise ships are. Angel is jumping up and down really.

"Brian really? We are going on a cruise?"

"Yes, babe, it is another thing I should have done with you."

Angel jumps in Brian's arms.

"Oh, my God, babe! You just don't know how much this means to me."

"I know, baby. It was your dream."

"Well, it's a dream come true."

Brian had booked them on one of the newest big ships that Royal Caribbean had. Angel had the best time of her life. She finally was able to experience what it felt like to have her man, her husband, with her on a cruise ship and not be a third wheel. Angel was so at peace. She was very grateful for Brian doing all of this to make it so special. But most of all, Angel was so thankful that God showed favor over her and Brian for allowing the pass to not hinder their future for blessing them, in spite of their circumstances. Angel believed when you let go and let God watch, how he blesses you. Angel waited on God, and God gave her more than what she had ever expected. That is being able to surrender, to release, to trust, and to forgive. God's love is everlasting. Brian and Angel both seek God's love first and he rewarded them at the end with peace.

ACKNOWLEDGEMENTS

I like to thank God for the inspiration, for being my lifeline. Without Him, I would be nothing. I like to thank my children Chris, ZaShea', and Malik for their support, love, and for believing in me. You guys are my world. To my family and friends for believing in me and pushing me to finally write a book—thank you all for the encouragement. To my daughter-in-law Jaseele, you really give me life and your words of encouragement mean a lot to me. To Iyana, I can't begin to express my gratitude for the hours of you listening to me go on and on, thank you! To Medda, my dear close friend, I have no words for what you mean to me. You are truly a blessing from God. I thank you for everything, for being in my life. To my two co-workers Janette and Destiny, you two have been my foundation at work. Your support and friendship mean the world to me. Thank you! To Jerico, I thank you for seeing the lady in me, for your words of encouragement, for allowing me to see the Queen that I am. For pushing me to honor myself, to not just except anything from a man. You showed me that I deserve true love and time. This book wouldn't be if it wasn't for God and you!

WITH EVERY BREATH, HE TOOK MY SOUL

By Niecie Hammond

BIOGRAPHY

Niecie Hammond was born in Columbus, Ohio but raised up on a military base in Ft. Leonard Wood, with her mother, father, sisters and brothers. She lives in Marietta, GA, where her 3 children and grandchildren reside as well. She is currently in the law enforcement field and is seeking her bachelor's degree in psychology.

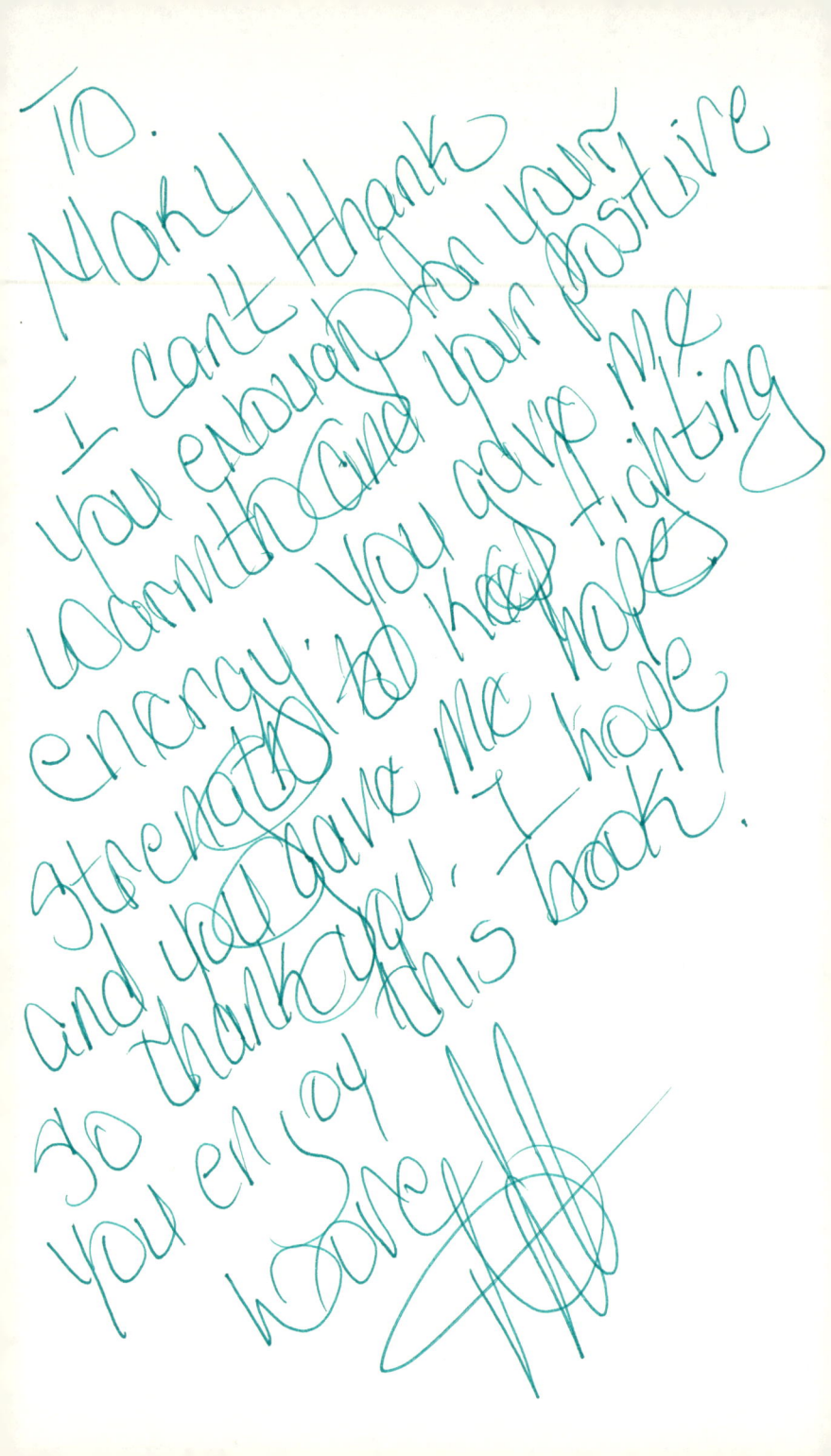

To.
Mary
I can't thank you enough for your warmth and your positive energy. You gave me strength to keep fighting and you gave me hope. So thank you. I hope you enjoy this book.

Love,

Made in the USA
Columbia, SC
06 May 2021